ANOTHER CHANCE

Firefly Inn Book 1

ANNIE DOBBS

* * * * * * * *

When newly widowed Virginia Flynn turns an abandoned mansion into the Firefly Inn, she never dreams that the inn's other-worldly guest will play a mysterious part in her plans, starting right with her first visitor....

Stacy Brighton left her hometown on the coast of Maine ten years ago for bigger and better things and never looked back. But when her father dies unexpectedly, she's forced to return. She won't spend a minute longer than she has to, though. That town is full of bad memories and she doesn't want to see any of the people she left behind, especially not Reid Callahan.

Reid Callahan never wanted anything more than to live his life in Rocky Point. He loves the simple, small-town life and has proudly grown his small lobstering business into one of the premier restaurants in the area. He's made a good life for himself but something seems to be missing. And when Stacy comes back to town, he knows exactly what it is. Too bad Stacy has no intention of staying... or does she?

Even their growing attraction might not be enough to soothe old wounds and when their worst fears take root, one of them may have to sacrifice everything they thought they wanted in order to give their hearts another chance.

CHAPTER 1

Welcome to Boulder Point, Maine!

Stacy Brighton gripped the steering wheel of her mid-sized rental car tighter as she passed the familiar sign at the edge of the small coastal town on her way out of the trailer park where her mother lived. It had been nearly a decade since she'd been back. The one place she'd never planned to return to.

Looked like not much had changed since she'd left. Same quaint, if not somewhat empty, main street, same small shops, same feeling of dread in her chest.

She took a deep breath and watched her speed carefully. These small towns were notorious ticket traps for tourists. The town's tiny police department made three-quarters of its quota in these summer months alone, a fact she hadn't forgotten since leaving for college ten years ago. Even after four years of school and another six in a high-powered job with a prestigious event-planning firm in Columbus, Ohio, she still remembered how easy it was to get caught speeding on this little stretch.

The fact her father was gone still hadn't fully registered yet. From the moment she'd received the frantic call from her sister, Brenda, a few days ago, Stacy had felt as if she were walking around in a daze. Old memories and fresh heartache had chased her all the way from Ohio back to Maine, worsening once her plane touched down two hours earlier.

Now, she fought hard to keep her hands from shaking on the steering wheel and swallowed hard against the knot of sadness in her throat.

So much water under that bridge, so much regret ...

Stacy accelerated and continued toward the town's new bed-and-breakfast, where she'd booked a room for her weeklong stay. Her mother had wanted Stacy to stay with her at the family's double-wide, but she just couldn't — despite the fact it would give her more time to catch up with her mother and Brenda and her cute little nephew, Sammy, whom she hadn't seen since his birth. Hard to believe the kid would be four years old now. The last time Stacy had spent time with him, he was just a baby.

So many memories. So much time lost ...

Her heart squeezed and her chest ached with remembrance of the town. She'd had a lot of good times here. A lot of horrible times too. But in the end, choosing to live in Columbus had been the right decision for her. Her dreams and career aspirations were too big for such a small town. She'd needed to get out, to spread her wings, to fly as high as her talent and ambitions would take her.

And it had all been worth it.

Hadn't it? She slowed as she rounded another curve in the road, and the knot of tension between her shoulder blades tightened to the point of pain as she passed another familiar sight.

The Boulder Point Cemetery. Weathered, crooked headstones jutted from the ground like sentinels, and dappled sunlight glinted through the pine branches above, lending the whole area a mystical quality. Two days from now, her father would join these departed souls in their eternal rest. She blinked back the sting of unshed tears. Crying wouldn't help her get things settled with the estate. She needed to be strong for her mother. She was always the strong one.

Flashes of her father's face — handsome, smiling, kind — filled her mind before she secured them away again. Shoulders slumped, she continued onward. She couldn't think about the fact she'd not made it home to see him. His death had been sudden, and she'd thought there would be plenty of time. He would've understood her need to work, her need to stay focused on her life and career in Columbus, especially after all he'd been through with losing his job and the long stretch of unemployment that had followed. He would've understood why she'd not come home in years.

Wouldn't he?

Another face took her father's place in her mind, this one younger though still as handsome. The other reason she'd left this place, the other reason she'd not returned. Even after a decade, the wounds were still too raw, still too deep to forgive. She'd been such a naïve idiot, so in love that she couldn't — wouldn't — see what had been right in front of her face all along.

The road straightened, and Stacy gave her compact a bit more gas, putting the past behind her as best she could. She was a different person now. She'd gone from small-town girl to big-city success story. The firm she worked for had assigned her exclusively to one of its biggest clients — a posh five-star hotel in Columbus with world-class amenities and a long list of top-tier guests. She'd single-handedly brought in more revenue for her company and her client than anyone else in her firm. All before her thirtieth birthday.

She'd also gone from being a naïve, besotted fool to savvy and world-wise.

Now she wouldn't waste years on a man who had been more loyal to someone else. One whose ambition didn't match hers. Who'd been content to stay in this nothing town and who had not even cared enough to contact her after she left Boulder Point. Not a single time in ten years. Not once.

Stacy lowered the driver's-side window as she drew closer to the cliffs along the edge of town and inhaled deeply of the Atlantic Ocean. The exhilarating scents of salt and warm sand awakened her senses in a way nothing else ever had. She'd forgotten how wonderful those smells were, so different from the diesel fuel and constant noise back home in Ohio.

Maybe after she settled into her room at the inn, she'd take a walk down by the shore. That had been one of her favorite things to do growing up, and she'd missed it more than she realized.

One final hairpin curve in the road had her hitting the brakes as she rounded the sharp turn, the wind from the open window whipping her hair into her face and ...

HONK!

Stacy jerked the steering wheel hard as the sickening screech of metal scraping metal rang through her ears. A navy-blue pickup truck sideswiped her tiny white compact before stopping several feet behind her car. Breath panting loudly in the deafening silence, Stacy gripped the steering wheel tightly as her vehicle veered to a stop along the berm. For a moment, she sat stunned. Bright sun streaked in through her open window, prickling her skin and only adding to the flush of adrenaline flooding her system.

Tentatively, she tested all her extremities one by one. Everything seemed intact and working properly. She rolled her neck and shoulders. They seemed okay too, if a bit stiff. She'd be sore tomorrow, probably, but alive.

What about the other driver? She raised her gaze to the rearview mirror in time to see the driver of the truck climb out and head toward her car. With the glare from the sun, she couldn't see the guy's face, only his tall, broad form. Stacy's mind raced. She should grab her license and registration. She should grab her mace in case the stranger decided to get violent. She should call the police.

She jumped out of the car, ready to defend herself or do battle over the damage. Then she froze in place, her mouth hanging open as she recognized the man. Reid Callahan. The one person she hoped to never see again. The man who'd ripped out her heart and shredded it like last year's phone bill.

"Stacy Brighton?" he said, sounding as incredulous as she felt.

Reid had filled out nicely over the years, his black T-shirt and faded jeans showing off an impressive build of muscles and lean sinew. His dark-brown hair gleamed with hints of copper, and his gray eyes were still far too perceptive for her comfort. A hint of dark stubble shadowed his chiseled jaw.

Her pulse thundered. He was as attractive as ever, maybe even more so since the years had given him an air of mystery and melancholy. Except he was still wearing the old T-shirt and jeans. The hallmark of someone without a future. He was still the same old townie.

If she'd had any fond memories of this town, they evaporated with the sight of him.

REID CALLAHAN TRIED to keep his face blank, even though his heart was drowning in a sea of emotion. He'd tried hard in the last decade to forget the woman who now stood in front of him. The woman who'd ripped out his heart and stomped it beneath her tiny stiletto heels.

Unfortunately, his now-dented truck and the fact Boulder Point was a small town would make that pretty much impossible.

"I wondered if you'd make it home for your father's funeral," Reid said, crossing his arms. "Nothing else seemed important enough to get you to come back."

Stacy snapped her mouth shut, her eyes narrowing in an expression he recognized. She was pissed off. His comment had hit home. Good. Served her right.

She crossed her own arms over her chest, mirroring his posture. "Reid. How are you? And Gabby?"

"Fine. Thanks for asking," he grated out.

Reid prided himself on his ability to stay calm. He always tried to lend a helping hand when needed, give back to those who'd helped him in life, strived to make the world a better place one day at a time. But damn if Stacy Brighton didn't make that hard.

She knew just which buttons of his to push for maximum effect. Always had.

That was one of the things he'd loved about her.

It was also what had torn them apart.

His normal composure evaporated in her presence, had from the first glimpse of that honey-blond hair through the window, but he'd told himself no way it was Stacy. After all, she'd run far and fast from Boulder Point, and away from him all those years ago. Made him almost envy her dead father for having the power to draw her back home.

Years ago, Reid had dreamt he and Stacy would be together forever. But she'd asked him for the impossible. He could never leave his brother and father, even if it was to be with Stacy. He'd tried to explain, but she'd assumed he was staying for another reason. The fight they'd had the last time he'd seen her hadn't been pretty.

Probably just as well. Boulder Point had everything Reid ever wanted, but the town wasn't big enough for Stacy. She would never have been happy here, and he doubted he would have been happy anywhere else. Then again, had he truly been happy here since she'd left?

Now, here she was again, careening into his world and threatening to destroy the new life and peace he'd created. He couldn't let her do that. Couldn't let her break his heart again. He frowned and cleared his throat, looking away from her too-pale face that made him care too much. "Sorry to hear about your father. He was a good man."

She relaxed a bit, but her hazel eyes remained wary. "Thanks."

Stacy's quiet, husky tone sucker punched Reid right in the gut, same as it always had, even all these years later. He kicked a pebble with the toe of his work boot and glanced back at his truck. The driver's-side door was marred good. Right over the decal he'd had installed a week ago for his new business venture, Callahan's Catering.

Sidling past him, Stacy teetered across the dirt shoulder of the road in her sandals and walked to his truck. "Is this your vehicle?"

"Yep." Did she think he was too poor to afford his own truck?

"You run a catering business?"

"Among other things."

"Huh." She gave a little shrug, looking away again fast. "You always did like to cook."

Memories of the two of them in the kitchen — him showing her how to make scones and doing more kissing than baking, her tasting of strawberries and sweetness — swamped his overstressed mind. Angry with himself for remembering, he ignored the warmth flooding his veins.

She was here for her father's funeral. She would be leaving again soon.

And she certainly wasn't here to see him.

Reid shook his head and sighed. "We need to exchange information. For the insurance companies."

"Of course." She hurried back to her rental, pulled the vehicle's registration from the glove box, then fished inside her expensive handbag for her license. The purse probably cost more than his monthly mortgage payment.

"Here," she said, turning back to him.

He jotted down her information before giving the paperwork back. "Guess our insurance agents will hash it out from here."

"Yeah. I have insurance on the rental, so ..." She shrugged and held a hand over her eyes to shield them from the bright summer sun.

They stared at each other across the expanse of a few feet, the silence awkward. Before she'd driven off to college and never looked back, they'd talked for hours about their hopes and dreams, about the future, about how they might marry and start a family.

Given her fancy clothes and snooty attitude, she'd moved on from all that a long time ago. Reid had thought he'd gotten past it too. Except now, seeing Stacy again, all those stupid emotions came rushing back like a tsunami, pulling him under.

"I should, um, get going," she said, opening her dented car door.

"Yep." He nodded, backing toward his truck. He'd been on his way to an important meeting with his catering crew. Yet nothing seemed more important now than taking in the sight of Stacy Brighton, all grown up and sparkling like a new penny. "I need to go too."

"See you around, Reid." She broke away first, same as before, climbing into her car and taking off, leaving him to watch her vehicle fade in the distance, just like the day she drove off to college and never bothered to contact him again.

Finally, he took a deep breath and got back in his truck, a persistent ache in his chest. This was ridiculous. He was a grown man, a successful entrepreneur in his own right. He needed to forget all about seeing his old flame and get back into gear on his business.

Reid pulled away from the berm in a spray of gravel.

Stacy hadn't wanted him bad enough to stay back then, and judging by the way she'd just acted, he knew she sure as hell didn't want him now.

CHAPTER 2

Stacy's thoughts swirled as she drove to the Firefly Inn. Of all the people in Boulder Point to smash into today, it would have to be Reid Callahan. The one person she'd hoped most to avoid.

Talk about fate having a sick sense of humor.

She'd been so flustered after the accident she hadn't even looked at the damage to her rental. A glance revealed the side mirror dangling from a few colorful wires. Each time she slowed for a stoplight, it smacked against the side of the car. Thankfully, she'd paid extra for the insurance coverage from the rental company.

Despite the collision, her thoughts continued to focus on Reid — the man who'd once been the center of her universe. Warmth still sparkled through her traitorous system from being near him. Seemed time and distance had done nothing to lessen his effect on her.

The light turned green, and she continued weaving her way along the cliffs overlooking the Atlantic Ocean. Ahead, the inn perched near the edge of a bluff, looking far different from the last time she'd seen it. When Stacy had lived in Boulder Point, the old house had been vacant for decades. But as she pulled into the little gravel lot in front of the stately Colonial-style two-story bed-and-breakfast, it was obvious the place had undergone serious renovations.

The home's peeling paint had been replaced by a soothing cerulean blue, and the aging, crooked shutters had been straightened and updated to a gleaming bright white. Even the wraparound porch had been replaced, all the broken balusters fixed and coated in alternating shades of white and gray.

Stacy cut the engine and got out, wincing slightly at her first sight of the scraped paint and exposed metal on the driver's-side door. She pulled her suitcase from the trunk then clicked the button on her key fob to lock the car before climbing the stairs to the stately char-coal-colored front door and ringing the bell.

A woman answered — about six inches shorter than Stacy and in her sixties. Thin, with bobbed silver hair and sparkling blue eyes full of mischief, she looked ready to get to work in her faded jeans and white T-shirt. The woman smiled kindly and extended her hand. "Hello. You must be Stacy Brighton. I'm Virginia Flynn, owner of the Firefly Inn."

"Nice to meet you, Mrs. Flynn," Stacy said.

"Oh please, call me Ginny." She gestured Stacy inside the foyer.

The interior had undergone significant change as well, sporting warm earth tones and freshly buffed honey-gold hardwood floors. Only the original mahogany paneling remained, along with the scroll-work bannister and carved newel post of the staircase.

Stacy had sneaked into the old place with Reid a few times while in high school. She remembered that most of the light fixtures had been shattered. Those too had been replaced, with gorgeous stained glass, their light casting a cheery glow. Quite a difference from the shabby, run-down eyesore she remembered.

"Wow! This place looks lovely," Stacy said. "When I was younger, it used to be quite a mess. You've done a beautiful job with the restorations."

"Thank you." Ginny took her suitcase and set it aside. "There's still a lot more that needs to be done, but it's shaping up nicely. You're actually my first guest."

"Really? I'm sure I won't be your last."

"You might want to save your accolades until after I've shown you around." Ginny laughed. "We're not even fully staffed yet. I've hired a cook and a couple of housekeepers to help me clean the rooms, but until I start turning a profit, most of the work is done by yours truly."

"That's a large undertaking for one person, isn't it?" Stacy asked, following her into a comfy sitting room decorated in beachy pastels of light green and pink.

"Yes." Ginny's expression turned sad as she walked to an ornately carved whitewashed fireplace. "But I've gotten used to doing things myself since my husband, Donald, passed away. This bed-and-breakfast was our dream. Since he died, I've been on my own ..." She traced her fingertips lovingly over the mantel before facing Stacy again, her smile a bit too bright. "But enough about the past. Let me show you the rest of the first floor."

Stacy understood the tightness around the other woman's eyes, the sorrow in her tone, and couldn't help wondering if Ginny's husband had died slowly or unexpectedly, like Stacy's father. Loneliness and regret ached inside her once more. The only time Stacy had come close to a love like the one Ginny seemed to have shared with her husband had been

Reid. But his loyalty to his precious Gabby had ruined any chance they had of forever.

Ignoring the niggle of emptiness inside her, Stacy followed Ginny through the dining room. She'd moved on, chosen a career and success over marriage and children. Everything had worked out for the best. She'd gotten what she wanted.

Hadn't she?

"What do you think?" Ginny asked, stepping into a well-appointed chef's kitchen.

Stacy forced her mind back to the tour. "It's great."

"Are you all right?" Ginny frowned slightly. "You seem a bit upset."

"Sorry. I'm a bit distracted with my father's upcoming funeral. Then I had a minor fender bender on the way here," she said, taking the seat Ginny offered her at the large butcher-style kitchen table. The floor was a lovely black-and-white tile, she noticed absently. "It's all left me flustered, I suppose."

"I'm so sorry for your loss." Ginny patted her hand. "Let me make some tea. That always helps me feel better. Do you need to see a doctor after your accident?"

"No, no. I'm fine. We didn't even call the police." Pictures of Reid, standing in the sun and looking entirely too handsome for his own good, flickered through her beleaguered brain. "It's all good."

"If you say so, but you'll be sore tomorrow. It's always worse the day after. I've got aspirin and ibuprofen on hand if you need any."

"Thanks." Having someone care for her for a change was nice. Stacy was used to doing the pampering — of her clients.

"No problem." Ginny set the kettle on the stove and fired the burner. "While we wait for that to boil, let me show you to your room."

"That sounds wonderful."

They climbed the wide wooden staircase, the steps creaking slightly under their weight. Stacy put her hand on the carved banister, the wood silky smooth from years of use and polishing. How many people had walked up these same steps? The house had to be almost two centuries old, and she found herself wondering about the families that had lived here.

A deep voice whispered something unintelligible behind her, and Stacy whirled around. No one was there.

"Did you hear someone?" she asked.

Ginny frowned, but Stacy noticed she was looking behind them too. "We're the only ones here, dear. I think it was just the stairs creaking."

They stopped on the second-floor landing, halting before a large oval window that overlooked a field of wildflowers beside the house. In the summer, Stacy remembered, that field lit up with fireflies. She and Reid used to chase them, trapping them inside old Mason jars. The fireflies were magical, and so had been her time with Reid. *Had* been.

Back then, they'd imagined this old place was haunted. Later, as teenagers, they'd sneaked in on a dare. In fact, Reid had given Stacy her first kiss outside this house. She'd thought she'd seen a ghost looking out this same oval window and leapt into Reid's arms. One thing had led to another and ...

Stacy shook off the memories and followed Ginny to her room. It smelled of lemon furniture polish and fresh sea air and was gorgeously decorated in white linen and lace. An enormous carved mahogany four-poster bed sat in the middle of the room, flanked by a cozy sitting area and a desk near the windows, which overlooked the ocean. Ginny had left the window open, and the ocean breeze fluttered the eyelet lace curtain gently.

Ginny went back downstairs and returned with Stacy's suitcase then backed out the door. "I'll leave you to unpack and see you downstairs for tea once you finish."

Back in the kitchen, Ginny took a seat at the table once more. This room had been the first she'd renovated after Donald's death. When they'd first toured the property before buying it, the whole house had been inhabited by mice. Once she'd made the decision to open the inn by herself, her first step had been to bring in the exterminators. Her second had been to have the contractors rip up and replace all the original tile in this room. They'd managed to replace it with something pretty close to the original, which made her happy.

The kettle whistled, and she got up to grab cups and saucers from the mahogany Victorian-style cabinet near the sink. The stainless-steel countertops gleamed in the afternoon sunshine, and she couldn't help thinking how much Donald would've loved this place.

A now-familiar sadness choked her throat, and Ginny blinked back tears as she placed two floral china cups and saucers, sugar cubes, milk, and a selection of tea bags on the table. The delicate cups had come from a local antique shop, their intricate roses-and-vines pattern so lovely she'd just had to buy them.

It was the little touches, Donald had always said, that made a hotel a home away from home. They'd owned several properties like this over the years, but nothing compared to Ginny's sense of accomplishment from this inn.

I did it, Donald. All on my own.

The joists in the ceiling above her creaked from Stacy's steps. Ginny smiled. Her first guest. A nice gal too, if a bit troubled. She saw it in the girl's eyes — conflict and unresolved pain. Two things Ginny knew about as well. Rambling on about Donald's death had been a mistake, though, no matter how deep the wound still ran. She'd do best to heed her late husband's advice of letting the guests talk while she listened.

Ginny opened a nearby drawer full of linen napkins then stopped short.

A pair of cute antique ceramic chef salt and pepper shakers sat on the windowsill over the sink. She'd found a whole collection of them, along with other pieces of furniture and dishes, when she'd first moved into the house. Problem was, she could've sworn she'd placed those on the table earlier.

She chuckled to herself and put them back on the table. Then again, her memory wasn't so good these days. Maybe she'd moved them and forgotten. After all, she was the only one here. Who else would've moved them?

Stacy came downstairs and into the kitchen a short while later, looking a bit more refreshed, with a fresh layer of powder hiding the smattering of freckles over her nose. Her outfit was a tad fancy for this part of rural Maine, but the poor thing had just lost her father. That certainly explained the lingering sadness surrounding the girl, and her quiet manner.

"Everything okay with your room?" Ginny asked.

"Yes, thank you." Stacy studied the kitchen. "We always thought this place was haunted when I was a kid."

Ginny's smile faltered slightly as her gaze flicked to the salt and pepper shakers. "Really? Well, I've been here for months now and haven't seen any signs of a ghost."

"That's good." They sat at the table, and Ginny poured them each a cup of water from the kettle. Stacy looked as if she needed a good friend, and Ginny was happy to oblige.

"Tell me about your father," she said. "Were you close?"

Stacy sighed, selecting a packet of Earl Gray. "I hadn't seen him in a while. My job in Columbus keeps me busy, so I don't make it home very often. My family used to live in a nice home not far from here, but then Dad got laid off from his corporate job, and we moved to the local trailer park." She stared down into her cup. "It was hard for him to find work, with the recession. He ended up as the seafood department manager at the grocery store."

"Oh dear," Ginny said, sensing the girl's embarrassment. "Still, that sounds like a good, honest job."

"Not everyone sees it that way," Stacy said. "I got bullied a lot in school because of it. I suppose that's part of the reason I couldn't wait to get out of Boulder Point. I wanted to get away from all that negativity."

"And did you?" Ginny asked, taking a sip of her lemon-chamomile tea.

"Yes." Stacy smiled. "I'm an event planner for a PR firm in Ohio. I love my job. I hate being away from it, even for a week."

"Still, that's not much time after a death," Ginny said. "When Donald died, there was so much paperwork to contend with, so many things to handle that crept out of the woodwork. Thankfully I had attorneys to help me sort through it all."

"I've never had anyone close to me die." Stacy frowned. "Hopefully it won't be too involved. I'd hate to leave my mom and sister to sort through the mess alone. I feel bad enough that I never got to say goodbye to my dad."

Ginny narrowed her gaze, feeling the same twinge

of regret in Stacy's voice deep inside her. What she wouldn't give for one more day with her beloved Donald or her dear parents or siblings. Even the baby girl who'd died moments after Ginny had given birth. "Well, as someone who's older and perhaps a smidge wiser, my advice is to make the most of whatever time you have. Family is important, and you never know when it could all disappear. You may never get another chance."

Stacy's cell phone buzzed from the pocket of her designer blazer, and she pulled it out to frown at the screen. "I'm so sorry, but I have to take this."

"No problem." Ginny waved her out of the room. She started to clean up, first putting the tea selection back in the pantry, and then turned as a scraping noise issued from the sink. Stunned, she stared at the sill below the window.

The salt and pepper shakers were back in their spot again.

CHAPTER 3

"Hey, Bren." Stacy leaned against the dark paneling of the hallway, doing her best to keep her tone light as she spoke to her sister. "What's up?"

"Hey, Stace. Tommy said he'd watch Sammy tonight. I thought maybe we could have dinner and catch up, just us girls. What do you say?"

"Oh, uh, okay." Stacy wasn't sure she was up to seeing half the town in Boulder Point's favorite pub, especially after her earlier run-in with Reid. "What about Mom? Maybe we should eat with her at the trailer tonight? I only got to visit with her for a couple of hours right after I got in today."

"She's going out with friends," Brenda said. "I already checked. Please, I love my husband, but he's driving me up the wall right now with his attentiveness. He's only trying to be helpful, I know. But I need some time away. Please."

"Well …" Stacy stared down the hall into what looked like a library, frowning. She would've sworn someone just passed in front of those windows, but she and Ginny were the only two people at the inn, and Ginny was still in the kitchen. She headed to the room to investigate as she talked. "I guess we could."

"Thank you," Brenda said. "I know just the place."

"Please, not the old pub, okay?" Stacy peeked her head in through the doorway at the end of the hall. The library had apparently not made the renovation list yet. Dusty bookshelves lined the walls, half-filled with tattered books, some with fractured spines.

The stagnant air smelled of musty paper, and dust motes swirled through the rays of sunlight. A few pieces of tarp-covered furniture scattered the room, and a long table stretched down the middle of the space. Several scrolls were stacked in the center — blueprints, maybe? Stacy moved closer to look, and a slight breeze from the open window stirred the hair at the nape of her neck. Squawking seagulls and the soothing purr of waves on the shore lulled her to relax. No one was here. It must've been a figment of her exhausted imagination.

"No problem. I'll take you to the new place. Just

opened." Brenda asked, "What time should I pick you up, sis? You're staying at the Firefly, right?"

"Yep." Stacy rubbed her tired eyes. She'd like nothing more than to turn in early, but Ginny's words from earlier filtered through her head.

Family is important, and you never know when it could all disappear ...

"How about seven?" Stacy said. "I don't want to be out too late."

"Sounds good. You're going to love the Salty Dog," Brenda said. "Tommy and I checked it out a few weeks ago. They have the best micro-brews in town."

Brenda had been smitten with her husband, Tommy Stone, since the first day she'd seen him in third grade. He was a great guy and a wonderful father to their son, Sammy. Stacy couldn't have asked for a better brother-in-law.

"The Salty Dog, huh? Sounds interesting." Stacy exhaled. Beer wasn't exactly her drink of choice, but now that she was back in rural Maine, pickings were slim. "Okay, see you then."

"See ya soon, Stace."

STACY WALKED into the Salty Dog Pub and Grill with

Brenda. She'd changed out of her black power suit in favor of a more Boulder Point-appropriate outfit of jeans, T-shirt, and flip-flops.

The pub was more upscale than she'd expected, its seaside vibe almost trendy. And she almost hadn't recognized her sister when she'd come to pick her up. They Skyped from time to time, and Brenda and Tommy had brought Sammy out to see her in Columbus when he'd been just a baby, but it had been a few months since they'd last talked.

Brenda had cut her blond hair into a short pixie that suited her well and brought out the green in her eyes. At least the freckles they both shared had stayed the same. Brenda never tried to hide hers beneath layers of expensive makeup and powder as Stacy did, and her skin practically glowed with happiness.

A friendly hostess showed them to a table near the floor-to-ceiling windows overlooking the coast, taking their drink orders before leaving. The pub was relatively quiet, which helped Stacy relax and talk freely. "I still can't believe Dad's gone."

"Me neither," Brenda said, straightening her short-sleeved fuchsia sweater. "At least he didn't suffer. The doctors said the massive heart attack killed him before he knew what hit him."

A wave of grief and guilt so strong it nearly

dropped Stacy to the floor overwhelmed her. "I'm so sorry I wasn't home more over the years, but ..."

"But you had to leave. After everything that happened after Dad got laid off. And you had bigger aspirations. And well ... there was that whole blowout with Reid." She reached over and took Stacy's hand. "We all understood. And we're all proud of you. Well, Mom and Dad and I are. Can't speak for Reid."

Stacy snorted and shook her head. "I ran into him earlier. Literally. Sideswiped his truck out on the highway. He's still the same old Reid. Still as closed-off and secretive as ever."

Brenda exhaled and narrowed her gaze. "Stace, maybe if you talked to him — "

"I did. Reid chose to stay here. He let me leave without even trying to stop me, so I'm sure he had something better here." She flexed her stiff fingers to release some tension, surprised that the thought of it still hurt so much. She'd been so naïve, wondering why Reid had made excuses for Gabby, especially with the way Gabby used to bully her. Buying his smooth words about how he felt sorry for Gabby and there nothing going on between them.

But then Stacy noticed Reid was spending a lot of time with Gabby. When she'd questioned it, he'd claimed that it wasn't what she thought. But after she left, she'd heard they were inseparable for a while, and even though Reid claimed he didn't want to leave town with her because of his father and brother, she suspected the real reason was Gabby.

Get it together girl. That was ten years ago. Shouldn't you be over it by now?

"Anyway, what does it matter now? That was a long time ago, and I've moved on."

"I think you all have." Brenda sat back as the hostess brought her pale ale and Stacy's white wine. "You know Gabby's married now. And not to Reid."

The news caught Stacy by surprise, but she did her best to hide it. Reid hadn't mentioned that earlier. *Figures. He's still keeping his secrets.* She took a sip of her wine, savoring the cool, earthy taste before swallowing hard. "Really?"

"Really. She's married to a guy by the name of Bruce Weaver. He moved here from Oregon about five years ago. Good man, and a great chef."

"Great." Her flat tone suggested the exact opposite. The last thing she wanted to do tonight was hash over old wounds. "What are we going to do about Mom? She can't stay in that beat-up old trailer alone, Bren. It's not safe."

"It's fine. You always took living there way harder than the rest of us," Brenda said. "Mom's kept the maintenance up real nice. It's the best-looking double-wide lot in the park."

"Maybe, but I still don't like the idea of her living there alone."

"You try to convince her to leave. She won't listen to me," Brenda said, perusing her menu. "Plus, Dad didn't leave her a lot of money. It's a nice park. Good people there. It'll be hard to find a place that nice somewhere else that she can afford."

Stacy scoffed. She was already footing most of the bill for their father's funeral. If it meant making sure her mother was safe, she'd chip in for a house in a better part of town. Still, given the sour look on her sister's face, now wasn't the best time to discuss it. She switched topics yet again, using her best Maine accent. "How's Tommy and my favorite nephew?"

"Hubby's great," Brenda said, giggling. "Working a lot at the mill to pick up extra money, but we're so happy, sis. And Sammy's ornery as ever. He's so excited to see his Auntie Stace."

"Aw." Warmth flooded her system as the years fell away. Once more, they were back in high school, discussing the latest town gossip and the good folk of Boulder Point. Perhaps coming out with Brenda tonight hadn't been such a bad idea after all.

Brenda fell quiet at last as she picked at the bright-yellow label on her bottle. "Do you ever think about moving back here, sis? You live so far away, and I really miss you."

"I miss you guys too." Stacy sighed, her heart aching. "It's just hard. I have a great career. Plus there's a lot of baggage here for me and — "

Before she could say anything more, a deep, masculine laugh interrupted her speech.

Reid.

Stacy glanced over to see him at the bar, talking to a bleached blonde who appeared to be drunk, if the way she swayed precariously on her stool was any indication. He looked none the worse for wear from their earlier collision. Stacy already felt a telltale ache in her muscles. Ginny had been right. She would be sore tomorrow.

It should be illegal for a man to have treated her so badly and still look so good. Not that she pined for him. Not only had he not been honest with her, but things would have never worked between them. Stacy had ambitions, bigger aspirations than Boulder Point, while Reid ... well, he was a hometown boy still hanging around in the same bars with the same people he'd hung with in high school.

Brenda glanced over her shoulder and then snorted. "Speaking of baggage, there's Gabby now."

Stacy's gaze narrowed. Gabby was a blonde now? Back in high school, she'd been a brunette. Now her hair was almost the same color as Stacy's. And there she was, hanging all over Reid. Just like old times. Stacy shrugged, pretending to be unaffected. She hunched down in her seat and peered past her menu to watch as Reid flirted with the now-married and very drunk Gabby.

"Are you hiding?" Brenda snorted. "Seriously, sis. I bet if you talked to him, you guys could work this out. You used to be so close."

"Yeah, well, things change. Besides, I gave him the chance to talk ten years ago. He didn't take it. Haven't heard a word from him since."

"Reid's a good guy, sis. Are you sure you weren't blowing things out of proportion?"

"Excuse me?" Stacy scowled. "You make it sound like the breakup was *my* fault, Bren."

"No, it's just that I don't think he had anything going with Gabby. Maybe you overreacted."

"Really? Then why didn't he come with me? No, there was something going on all right. He made his choice back then, and it looks like he's still making that same choice now."

Stacy slumped back in her seat and stared out the window at the lights of the fishing trawlers offshore in the twilight. Apparently Reid hadn't changed since high school. Yet another reason to avoid him while she was in town.

"I suppose Reid's still hanging around the docks, hauling lobster traps for a living? When he's not driving the catering truck."

"You have a lot to catch up on, sis," Brenda said, flashing a coy smile.

Reid helped Gabby from her stool then eased her toward the door. He looked over and caught Stacy's eye, and a flicker of surprise passed over his handsome face before he covered it fast beneath his usual layer of stoicism. He gave her an annoyed stare and backed out of the exit, Gabby in his arms.

Once they were gone, Stacy exhaled slowly and lowered her menu, staring at the tabletop. "He's still as irresponsible as I remember."

"Hardly, sis." Brenda swallowed a large gulp of her ale. "Reid's one of the most responsible guys in town these days. And one of the most successful."

"Yeah?" she said, disbelief riding her hard. When she'd left Boulder Point, Reid had been a lobsterman — loved hanging out at the docks and walking the beach. Not exactly the stuff of which business titans were made.

In her mind, the night she'd left town played like a

movie. Their fight in the street. The harsh words they'd said. The way he'd shut her out completely when she'd demanded he tell her the truth about Gabby Nelson. Why had he always sided with her when the girl obviously had it out for Stacy?

He'd claimed there was nothing between them. That he wasn't siding with Gabby. He had reasons but couldn't tell her what they were. He said she needed to trust him.

He claimed he needed to stay in Boulder Point, had to stay close to home and his family. That was what had really stung. She just wasn't important enough for him to leave Boulder Point. Especially not when Gabby was waiting in the wings to take over. She'd vowed then and there to prove to him and everyone else that she was important, successful, strong, and independent.

She'd driven out of Boulder Point that night with her head held high and never looked back.

"He started a restaurant a few years back," Brenda continued, drawing Stacy back to the present. "Now he owns three — the Salty Dog Pub, The Mariner, and The Tuckaway Grill. Plus, his new catering business on the side. They do some event setup too, everything from A to Z. Kind of like what you do in Columbus. I bet you two have more in common than you think, sis."

"I doubt it." Stacy stared out the window across the room, spotting Reid helping Gabby into the passenger seat of his pickup truck. A flash of the logo on his driver's-side door crossed her mind.

Callahan's Catering. Creating the Unforgettable, One Event at a Time.

She'd assumed the company belonged to his father and Reid only worked there.

Turned out Reid had made something out of himself after all.

Through the window, Stacy saw Gabby cling to him as Reid buckled her seat belt. Her chest pinched, not with sadness, but with ... *jealousy?* Nah. That was ridiculous. From the looks of things, what Reid had made out of himself tonight was an adulterer, if what Brenda had said about Gabby being married was true.

I can't tell you about Gabby, Sunshine. I'm sorry, but it's not my place ...

Not his place. Just a trick to get her to stop asking so he could avoid telling her what was really going on. Did he think she was that naïve? She rolled her eyes at his remembered pet name for her and knocked back the rest of her wine, hailing the waitress for a refill. "Well, with luck, I won't run into Reid or Gabby again while I'm here. Figures the last person I want to see is the one person I hit, right?"

Brenda cringed. "Actually, you'll see more of him than you think. I hired him to cater the memorial luncheon after Dad's funeral."

"What? Why?" Stacy gritted her teeth as her stomach sank. "Isn't there anyone else who can do it?"

"Not really." Brenda wrinkled her nose. "I'm sorry, sis, but it's a small town. And you said to hire the best person for the job when we spoke on the phone. He's by far the best in the area, and at the time, I figured it would give you both a chance to get reacquainted." Brenda threw her hands up in surrender at Stacy's glare. "We want the best for Dad, right? Besides, I had no idea you'd drive like a bat out of hell once you got here and run over everything in your path."

"It was an accident, like I said. I was distracted."

"Right. Whatever. I've ridden with you before, remember? I think living in that big city has given you road rage." She laughed and ducked as Stacy threw a wadded napkin at her head. "Before you start tossing the condiments, there's something else you need to know. Tommy has to work in the morning, and Sammy's got a doctor's appointment. Which means you need to meet with Reid to sort out the setup and menu for the memorial luncheon."

CHAPTER 4

"C'mon, Gabby. A little help here would be nice," Reid mumbled.

His passenger was so buzzed she was like a sack of soggy, limp noodles. No help at all. At least he'd managed to get her seat belt belted while she giggled and sang him an off-key rendition of the Miley Cyrus classic, "Wrecking Ball." Now that he thought about it, that song was the perfect accompaniment to Reid's disaster of a day. He shook his head as he started the engine, Gabby still humming along beside him. And to top off his craptacular evening, he'd seen Stacy again.

The way she'd glared at him on his way out of the pub left no doubt in his mind how she felt about their second encounter. It didn't help that Gabby had been there with him, all but hanging off him like a monkey

on a vine. Which told him she was still hurt by everything that had happened ten years ago.

For a long time, Reid had thought Stacy was The
One. He'd imagined being with Stacy for the rest of his
life. Then came the day she'd hightailed it out of
Boulder Point and out of his life forever. Turned out
he wasn't good enough. Sure, she'd asked him to come
with her, but what was he going to do, hang onto her
coattails while she went to college and then on to a big
fancy career?

Reid didn't have the money for college, and he was
his own man. No way he'd sit around the house or take
a job as a stocky somewhere and let Stacy provide for
him. The relationship never would have worked that
way. And when he hadn't been able to tell her about
his relationship with Gabby, Stacy had walked away
for good. Didn't even look back.

"Why so sad?" Gabby hiccupped then tipped sideways. Reid managed to catch her before she took a
header into the dashboard and pushed her back into
her corner of the seat, grateful the seat belt kept her
from slumping to the floor. Her smile took a downturn,
and her words slurred. "You're such a good guy, Reid.
How come you never got married?"

You.

Reid bit back the word and his resentment, forcing

a smile. "Bruce is a good guy. You're just going through a rough patch. You'll work it out." He glanced from the road ahead to her then back again. At least he hoped they would. They had two adorable toddlers, and he knew firsthand how destructive a crumbling marriage could be on kids.

Besides, Bruce Weaver was Reid's assistant and closest friend. Gabby helped him with the accounting and office work for the restaurants and catering business. If they split up, there went at least half his workforce. So, when Reid had seen Gabby alone at the bar, well past three sheets to the wind, there was no way he'd let her drive home.

Gabby sniffled in the seat beside him, tears running down her cheeks now. "Bruce hates me. We had a horrible fight and said horrible things to each other. All I want to do is get out of there."

He exhaled slowly and summoned all the patience he could before answering. "C'mon, Gabs. You of all people should know that walking away won't solve anything. You and Bruce are great together. If you love him, then you work it out. End of story. Leaving is for losers."

"Are you calling me a loser?" Gabby straightened and started to undo her seat belt before Reid stopped her.

"No. It was a poor choice of words. I'm sorry. Just please calm down, okay?" He got her settled before the light turned green.

"Fine."

As he drove past the trailer park, images of Stacy popped into his mind once more. If leaving *was* for losers, then what did that make him and Stacy?

His mother had left, walked out before he and his brother and father even knew what hit them. Stacy had left too, but he could never consider her a loser. She'd been his rock during the worst time of his life — the day his mother had left him and his father and his little brother. Her parents had become his surrogate family, and if it weren't for Stacy, he wasn't sure he'd have pulled through.

Then, as they'd grown older, she'd leaned on him too. After her father had lost his job and they had to move to the trailer park, Reid became Stacy's shoulder to cry on. He'd thought they'd always be there for each other. But then Gabby came into the picture, and the secrets he'd vowed to keep drove a wedge between them.

The night Stacy left town for college, he'd wanted so much to come clean, to tell her everything. It had damned near killed him not to. If he lived to be one hundred, he'd never forget the tears in her eyes, the knife of pain twisting in his heart, so deep he wasn't sure it would ever heal. She'd thought he was choosing Gabby over her, and there was nothing Reid could do or say to convince her otherwise.

He signaled then turned onto the quiet side street where Gabby and Bruce lived as her soft snores filled the interior of the truck. He hazarded another glance over and found her out cold, her head resting against the passenger-side window, her breath fogging the glass.

Reid gave a soft snort then shook his head, slowing for a stop sign. This neighborhood was nice. Lots of kids and dogs and white picket fences. Very family oriented. He had a place closer to town. Made it easier to get to work in the mornings, and he liked living closer to the action.

Maybe things had worked out for the best after all. Stacy had been accepted into a fancy college in another state, and he had his father and his little brother to consider.

Mikey had been only twelve at the time their mother had walked out on them. His father barely made enough then to cover the mortgage payments, let alone food and clothes for all of them. And Gabby, well, that was an entirely new situation dumped on him the summer between ninth and tenth grade.

No way could he have left them all behind to fend for themselves, as his mother had done. So Reid stayed behind. Not that it was such a horrible sacrifice in all ways. Truth was, he loved the coast and the simpler life small-town living provided. Stacy and he had both made their own ways in the world. Yep. Things had definitely worked out for the best.

Reid turned into the driveway, ignoring the squeeze of yearning in his chest.

On the bright side, at least Gabby hadn't hurled in his truck. That would've been wicked awful to clean. Reid shifted into park then glanced up at the modest, well-maintained ranch-style home.

Warm lights glowed through the curtains of the living room, meaning Bruce was home. That was good because, given Gabby's dead weight, he might need some help getting her into the house. The poor thing had her demons to battle, her own abandonment issues to deal with and conquer. Reid had tried to be there for her as best he could, but even he had his limits.

He got out and walked around to the passenger side, carefully opening the door and then reaching in to catch a comatose Gabby with one hand and hold her in place while he unbuckled her seat belt.

The insurance adjuster was coming in the morning to assess the damage to his truck. Hopefully, it would be an easy fix and he could move on without too many complications. That was how he liked things these days — uncomplicated.

Reid swung Gabby into his arms and closed the door with his hip. She wasn't that heavy, after all, at least not compared to the huge crates of supplies he was used to hauling around at the restaurants.

Making his way up the sidewalk to the front door, he briefly worried Bruce might be putting the kids to bed, but he answered at the first knock.

"Hey, man. Thank goodness she's okay. I was worried when she walked out before dinner," Bruce said, his expression a mix of grateful and exhausted. "It's been one of those days."

"No kidding," Reid said, passing Gabby off to her husband. From the moment Stacy Brighton had barreled around that corner and back into Reid's life, he'd known he was in trouble. Seeing her again had shaken him.

With her father's funeral in a few days, and the memorial luncheon afterward to plan, hopefully they could remain cordial until it was over. Then Reid could return to his uncomplicated life alone.

CHAPTER 5

That evening, Ginny stood on the second-floor landing of the inn, peering out the oval-shaped window at the field next door. Fireflies flickered and floated over the long grass like tiny fairy lights, so peaceful and enchanting. She sighed, smiling.

It was still early, only 9:00 p.m., but now that Donald was gone, she'd gotten in the habit of retiring around this time. With the inn to run, she had to be up before dawn. And now that she had her first guest, it was imperative she have breakfast ready on time tomorrow. In the hospitality business, you grabbed rest whenever you could find it.

From the floor below, Ginny heard the front door open and close, followed by the creak of footsteps in the hall. *Must be Stacy, back from her evening out.* Ginny didn't want to be one of those busybody innkeepers always sticking their noses into their guests' business, so she headed for her room. As she closed her door for the night, she hoped Stacy would find some happiness and closure while she was home in Boulder Point.

The girl had seemed so sad for one so young.

With Donald gone now, along with the rest of her family, Ginny needed a new outlet for her mothering instincts. She'd opened the inn, hoping it would keep her busy and ease the ache of loneliness, but she hadn't realized until today just how starved for companionship she'd been. Yes, she had her staff — the cook and the maids — but she'd hired them only a week ago and hadn't had a chance to bond with them yet.

She slipped off her robe and turned back the sheets on her bed then sat on the edge of the mattress to remove her slippers. No. She'd made the right decision opening this inn. Today had proved that. It would help fill the hole in her life left by Donald's death, with all the new people coming and going. It would also help keep her from getting too close to anyone.

Her poor heart had been battered one too many times from losing those she loved. Now she pictured herself content to keep things superficial, chatting with the future guests and wishing them well once they headed off to their real lives again. She'd always been a bit of a loner by nature anyway.

Besides, sometimes it felt as if this old place had a personality and life of its own. In several of the rooms, an inexplicable comfort came over her, enveloping her like a warm hug. And the salty sea air and crash of the waves helped soothe her soul.

Ginny shut the light on the nightstand and walked to the windows overlooking the gardens below the back of the inn. They were still a mess, but now that the interior of the house was mostly done, she'd start on the landscaping next.

A flash of movement caught her eye, and she squinted but spotted nothing out of the ordinary. Maybe a bird or a squirrel. Or worse, an overprotective hedgehog or skunk. She hoped she wouldn't have to deal with either of those. From up here, she could take in the true potential of the space below. The garden area was extensive, with a path looping along the edge of the cliff to give guests a gorgeous view of the ocean.

Donald would've loved that.

She sighed and headed to bed, her gaze drifting to the silver-framed photograph of him on her nightstand. Ginny frowned. When she'd placed that there, it had faced the bed. Now, it angled toward the window.

Maybe the new housekeeper, Emma, had moved it when she'd cleaned.

Except Emma didn't clean this room.

She climbed into bed and moved the photo to face her once more. Ginny liked waking up to Donald's smiling face each morning. It made it seem as if he was still here with her. She settled in with a sigh, snuggling into her pillow and drifting off to sleep.

CHAPTER 6

Stacy tossed all night, imagining her upcoming meeting with Reid. Yes, she'd told her sister to hire a good caterer to handle the luncheon after their father's funeral, but she'd never expected that caterer to be Reid Callahan. Or worse, that she'd be the one stuck working with him to arrange everything.

She huffed and rolled over, punching her pillow hard.

If she didn't know better, she'd think Brenda was up to something — trying to get her and Reid back together. There was no way that would happen, not after what he'd done.

But what exactly *had* he done? She really had no proof he'd been dating Gabby back then. After she left, maybe he had, but what was wrong with that? It wasn't as though Stacy hadn't dated anyone else in the past ten years. They'd broken up that night, each of them free to see whomever they wanted.

Brenda's comment about her overreacting rang in her ears. Had she been overreacting back then? She'd been young and immature. Maybe she had been too hard on Reid. He wasn't a liar, but she *knew* he was holding something back about Gabby. Then again, Reid had been young, too. Maybe his overactive hormones had simply caused him to make a mistake. It was so long ago it was stupid to hold a grudge about it now.

Even so, Brenda's subtle plan wouldn't work. There was far too much pain between them now, far too much time gone, for them to ever get back to where they were before she left town, wasn't there?

Grunting, she flopped back to her other side again.

Yep. There was. She had a career in Ohio, and Reid had one here. And then there was Gabby. She'd been shocked to see them together last night. The Reid she'd known wasn't one who would step out with a married woman. But it had been ten years, and people changed. Yep, too much time and too many changes for them to ever get back to where they'd been. She'd go to his restaurant, get in and get the plans for the luncheon settled, then get back to her life and responsibilities.

She cracked one eye open and glanced at the digital clock on the nightstand. Six thirty. The savory smell of bacon drifted from the kitchen downstairs, and Stacy's stomach growled. Because she wasn't doing much sleeping, might as well get up and face the challenges ahead. Brenda had scheduled the meeting with Reid for nine and had given Stacy directions to his other restaurant, The Tuckaway Grill, before they'd gone their separate ways last night. She'd said all Stacy had to do this morning was pick out the menu and go over particulars — like seating arrangements and table coverings. Easy enough, or should be, anyway.

Grumbling, Stacy got up and made her bed, then headed to the bathroom next door. After a quick shower and brushing her teeth, she returned to her room and studied the clothes she'd brought for the trip.

What did one wear to a meeting with the ex-love of your life? She considered dressing in her usual business garb of black suit, white blouse, and sensible shoes. But Reid had seen her in that same outfit yesterday when they'd had their little accident.

Nope. Casual was better, she decided. There was no reason to primp for Reid Callahan. She pulled on a pair of old faded jeans and a dowdy gray T-shirt that hung loose to her hips. Didn't bother with makeup at all, just slicked her damp hair back into a severe low ponytail before heading downstairs toward the source of those delicious smells. After all, her father had just died. She had no reason to celebrate, no one to impress.

Ginny met her at the bottom of the stairs, a slight frown on her pretty face.

"What's wrong?" Stacy asked once she reached the first floor.

"Oh, nothing. I thought I saw something moving around out there in the gardens." Ginny moved to a nearby window and pulled the curtains aside. She pointed to an overgrown rose bush, its thorns and leaves and few sparse flower buds all but obscuring the view to the ocean beyond. "Whatever it was, it's gone now."

"Huh." Stacy moved beside Ginny and peered outside. "Yeah, I don't see anything."

"It was probably just a rabbit." She let the curtain fall closed. "I haven't gotten around to sprucing up the gardens yet. I'd planned to restore them this summer, but then I booked a big wedding next month, so I guess I need to get on that quicker now, huh?" She guided Stacy toward the kitchen. "I was just coming to wake you. Maisie, my new cook, is preparing breakfast.

Think of it as a trial run. You can test things out and let me know what you like."

"Well, if everything tastes as wonderful as it smells, I'm sure I'll love it all." Stacy greeted the petite, thin woman cooking at the stove and sat at the table. The cook turned to face her, a spatula in one hand and pancake batter splattering the front of her white apron. Her sharp gaze was narrowed, and her bird-like features reminded Stacy of a crow. Smart and wily. Maisie's gray hair was pulled back into a tight bun on top of her head. Stacy guessed the woman was in her early seventies at least, though she moved with a spring in her step just the same.

Down here, the sizzle of the bacon blended with the rich aroma of freshly brewed coffee had her stomach rumbling anew. Through the large windows on one side of the kitchen, sunlight streamed inside.

"Why don't we go into the dining room to eat?" Ginny suggested. "It's more private."

"This is really lovely," Stacy said, following her into the room. The walls were covered in delicate Victorian-patterned wallpaper, and a large cobalt-blue, maroon, and gold-hued rug covered the center of the floor. A marble fireplace took up the far wall, and a glittering crystal chandelier hung from the middle of the ceiling.

The space was easily big enough to hold at least thirty people comfortably. Two rows of white-linen-covered tables lined the perimeter and gave the space a more restaurant-like feel. They chose a spot near the windows.

"Once I get everything situated, I plan to offer a buffet-style breakfast for guests." Ginny pointed toward a carved mahogany sideboard covered with silver warming trays. Labels read Bacon, Eggs, Pancakes, Potatoes, Gravy, and Biscuits. Crystal pitchers filled with juices and water, and a bottle of what looked like pure maple syrup, sat at one end. "I know you're the only one staying here at present, but Maisie can use the practice."

Stacy filled her plate at the buffet. The food looked delicious, and she took healthy portions of eggs, bacon, and fresh fruit. Returning to the table, she sat down then stood again. "Forgot salt and pepper."

"Oh, there're shakers on every..." Ginny frowned at the empty center of their table. "That's strange. I made sure there was a set at each place earlier this morning."

"Looks like there's two on this next table." Stacy grabbed the extra set — a gorgeous porcelain pair with pink hand-painted roses circa 1900. The other set on the table were jaunty top hats, probably from the '30s. "These are so cute. Where'd you get them?"

"I found them when I moved in. A whole collection of them." Ginny sounded distracted, and she still stared at the center of their table. "Maybe Maisie or the housekeeper moved them."

"Well, I wouldn't worry about it," Stacy said around a bite of eggs. They were creamy and salty and perfect, with a tangy hint of cheddar cheese. "I do things like that all the time. Move things or put them somewhere and swear I'll remember, then I promptly forget. And how cool the original owners of the house left a stash of goodies behind. Looks like you found the perfect way to put them to good use."

"Yes." Ginny gave her a polite smile, though she still seemed flustered. "Um, if you'll excuse me, I need to check on something in the kitchen."

"Sure, don't let me keep you from your duties." Stacy waved with her fork as Ginny retreated. For a split second there, when she'd first come downstairs, she'd nearly confided in the woman about all her current issues — like how guilty she felt about not visiting her father more often, like seeing how happy Brenda was with her family and her life made Stacy question the joy of her own, like how seeing Reid Callahan again had set off alarms and dredged up memories she didn't want to remember.

Thankfully she'd stopped herself. She'd just met

Ginny, for goodness' sake. And the poor woman had enough stress of her own trying to run this place. She didn't need Stacy's problems to add to the bunch.

REID ARRIVED bright and early at The Tuckaway Grill. The place didn't open for lunch for a few more hours, but this was his main location and where his office was located. It also housed the conference rooms where he met with clients of Callahan's Catering. Gabby usually joined him for these meetings, but he'd called Bruce earlier and discovered she was still a hungover mess from her binge at the bar the night before, so he'd told the guy to keep his wife home this morning and let her sleep it off.

Besides, he was only meeting with Brenda Stone, and the Brightons were like his own kin. Nothing he couldn't handle by himself. Brenda was always so organized and on top of things, it should be a breeze.

He shrugged off his jacket then gathered the paperwork and questionnaires needed to get everything set up the way Brenda wanted for the memorial luncheon after the funeral. By the time he'd gotten it all ready and walked back out to the front of the restaurant to unlock the entrance, a car already idled outside. His heart plummeted. Instead of Brenda's van as he'd expected, it was Stacy's white rental.

She exited the dented compact, blue paint from his pickup marring the vehicle's side, then walked toward him, her steps slow and her gaze wary. She looked about as excited as he felt about their upcoming meeting. Dressed as she was in jeans and a T-shirt, she looked much younger and less uptight today, more like the girl he'd fallen in love with all those years ago. The buzz of nerves in his system transitioned quickly into an ache of longing before he tamped it down hard.

Nope. Not going there. Not now. Not ever.

As she got closer to the entrance, he noted the slight gray tinge to her complexion, the tightness around her mouth, the lack of sparkle in her pretty hazel eyes. That sparkle of warmth and merriment had once drawn him in like a moth to a flame. Now, understandably, it was dimmed beneath sorrow.

Stacy pulled open the door and blinked in the darker interior of the restaurant, squinting at him until her eyes adjusted. "Um, hey. Brenda sent me to deal with these arrangements because she has her hands full with Sammy and errands today."

"Right." The word squeaked out of Reid's constricted throat, and he coughed before trying again. "Right. No problem." He gestured for her to follow him toward the back of the restaurant. "I've got the conference room set up if you're ready to get started."

"Yep." As they walked side by side, Reid did his best to ignore the hint of her lily of the valley perfume. To this day, that fragrance made his heart twist with memories.

"I'm sorry again about your father," he said to fill the awkward silence. "And about the accident yesterday. Hope you're not too sore."

"I'm fine," Stacy said, looking anywhere but at him. "And thanks. For the condolences."

Inside the small conference room, they took seats on opposite sides of the four-person table. Beneath these brighter lights, he noticed she wasn't wearing makeup. The freckles across her nose and cheeks were more visible now, as were the mossy-green flecks in her eyes.

He swallowed hard and pulled out a copy of the standard catering contract he'd started initially with Brenda over the phone. "Your sister ordered lunch service for fifty guests, to be delivered and served at the banquet facility in the funeral home." He pointed to a clause on the third page of the contract. "If you look here, you'll see — "

A chair toppled over in the restaurant, landing with a loud clatter. None of the staff were due in for another hour yet. Frowning, Reid stood. "Sorry. Let me just see what's happening out there."

He stuck his head out the door of the conference room and found a bedraggled Gabby kneeling near the entrance, the contents of her purse scattered on the floor. He sighed, remembering how he'd been called to her rescue yet again the night before. He should be used to it by now, he supposed. That seemed to be his role in life — caretaker, protector, peacemaker, and diplomat.

He winced as Gabby cursed loudly then finished gathering her stuff and stomped into her office, slamming the door behind her.

He closed the door and returned to the table. Stacy looked up at him. "Problem?"

"No, just Gabby bungling her way through the restaurant."

Stacy looked away. "Hung over from your big drinking binge last night?"

He couldn't read the expression on her face, but her tone was filled with hurt and disbelief, and maybe even a little disgust. Did she think he'd been out *with* Gabby?

"I wasn't drinking with Gabby. She works for me and is married to my assistant. I just happened to be in the bar and wasn't about to let her drive like that.

Besides, Gabby isn't the person you think she is. If you knew more about it, then — "

"Then what?" Stacy asked, crossing her arms. "Then I'd understand why she bullied me and made fun of me after my dad lost his job? And why you seemed to always make excuses for her? Sorry, buddy, I don't think so."

He exhaled slowly, hoping to ease some of the tension knotting his muscles. This whole time, he'd thought maybe time and distance had softened some of Stacy's hard, stubborn edges, but apparently not.

He understood her frustrations, knew that his inability to explain his relationship with Gabby made her assume the worst about him, but dammit, he'd made a promise the night his mother had walked out of Boulder Point and out of his life. A promise to Gabby and to himself that he would never, could never break. Not for himself, not for his family, not even for the woman he'd loved more than life itself.

If his mother's departure had taught him anything, it was that your word was your bond. Break that, and everything fell apart.

His parents had given their word to each other to stay together forever. His mother broke her promise and destroyed so many lives in the process. He refused to carry that same burden, no matter how badly he yearned to tell Stacy the truth.

When it came to Gabby, though, Stacy had always been completely unreasonable. Nothing Reid ever said was enough to stop her from assuming the worst back then. Why bother trying now?

Instead, he summoned all his patience and went over the provisions of the contract with her then laid out the options for the next day — food choices, seating arrangements, serving staff, utensils, décor. While she made her choices from the lists, he couldn't help studying her again. Tiny lines now fanned out from the corners of her eyes. The corners of her full lips were turned down slightly too, as if she hadn't smiled in a long time. Perhaps city life didn't agree with her after all.

Then again, losing a parent was enough to send anyone into a grief spiral.

He wondered if she felt guilty for not coming home very often to visit her parents during her self-imposed exile, wondered if she missed Boulder Point and the ocean and the nature. The town was no Columbus, but to Reid it was the most beautiful place on earth.

Stacy finished checking off items then handed him back the paperwork. "There. I think I got everything

Brenda wanted. Could we possibly have chicken Parmesan as one of the entrees? It wasn't on the list, but perhaps as a special request?" Reid met her gaze and — it was as if they were eighteen again. Back when Stacy had been all wide-eyed and innocent, so happy and carefree. Then her mask of sadness fell back into place, and she looked away. "It was my dad's favorite."

Her voice cracked, and his heart broke. It took every ounce of willpower he possessed not to pull her into his arms, to tell her everything would get better, even if it wouldn't. To keep from reaching for her, Reid exhaled and clenched his hands into fists on the tabletop. "Um, sure. We can do that. Are there any other things you'd like that aren't on that list?"

Stacy glanced over the menu one more time, ignoring the subtext of his words. "Nope. I think that's it."

They signed the contracts, and Reid printed a receipt. Then she was out the door and headed back to her car. The whole meeting had taken less than half an hour, yet he felt as if he'd just gone twenty rounds with Muhammad Ali.

Alone, Reid went back to the conference room and collected the paperwork before heading to his office beside Gabby's. She still hadn't come out. He thought about knocking, checking on her, but loud snoring came through the door, so he decided to let her be.

He'd just switched on his computer when the bells above the entrance door jangled again and footsteps pounded across the hardwood floors, heading in his direction. Reid stood, thinking maybe Stacy had forgotten something, but moments later, his father, Jim, stood in his office doorway.

"Hey, son," he said. "Was that Stacy Brighton I passed in the parking lot?"

"Yep." Reid took his seat again behind the desk and typed in his password. "We're catering her father's memorial luncheon tomorrow."

"Huh." Jim glanced over his shoulder at the empty front area then back to his son. "Too bad about her dad. Your mom and I knew her parents. Stacy was always such a cute little thing growing up. Looks tense now. What happened?"

"Life happened." Reid shook his head. "Besides, city living makes everyone tense."

"Yeah, I suppose you're right." His father sat in the empty chair before the desk. "You and her ever make up after that fight you had before she left for college? You were pretty broken up afterward, but you seemed to have recovered okay. Just look at what you've built here in Boulder Point. You've done well for yourself."

Reid nodded but remained silent, staring at his screen as he typed in Stacy's choices for the next day. It hurt not being able to cover the black hole of emptiness Stacy had left inside him the day she'd left, but his father didn't need to know that. He'd had enough troubles with women to last their whole family a lifetime. After what his mother had done, all the lies, all the deception, all the heartache she'd caused ...

"Dang women," Jim continued. "You never know what they're thinking. One day everything's great and the future's bright, the next they leave and never come back."

Or they drop a bombshell that blows your world sky-high ...

Breath hitching, Reid deleted a line of botched type with shaking fingers and tried again.

As a kid, he'd been so naïve. Had always thought his parents had been happy. Then, when he'd turned ten and his brother was five, his mother had walked out, shattering his world. At the time, Stacy had been his saving grace. His father, however, hadn't been so lucky.

After the divorce, he'd become bitter and angry for a long time. Reid suspected the man still pined for his mother all these years later, despite what she'd done. And they'd never heard a word from her. She'd never even sent a note to let them know she was okay or explain her actions. Nothing.

Good riddance.

Reid pounded in the rest of Stacy's information, striking the computer keys with more force than necessary. The last thing he needed was another woman in his life who was ready to bail at the first sign of trouble, a woman who refused to believe in him enough to give him the benefit of the doubt. Despite his earlier pangs of sympathy for her, he was glad she was leaving soon after the funeral. In fact, the sooner she got on a plane and got out of town, the better.

He'd cater her father's memorial luncheon, be careful not to spend any more time around Stacy than was necessary, then get back to his regular life. No way would he end up like his father, angry and bitter and missing the woman he'd loved and lost for the rest of his life.

CHAPTER 7

Stacy drove away from The Tuckaway Grill feeling decidedly shaken. It had been harder then she'd thought to see him again. And disheartening that he was still defending Gabby. Still keeping their little secret, whatever that was.

She shook her head and slowed for a red light, reminding herself that what she'd once had with Reid Callahan was old news. No sense in rehashing it.

Staring out the window at the quaint shops lining Boulder Point's main drag, she felt a bit better. Most of the stores looked the same as they had the day she'd left, except where there used to be many vacant store-fronts, now there were only a few. Most of them looked to have a new coat of paint or an awning or two. A bittersweet ache of nostalgia squeezed inside her. It was almost as if all the years had fallen away,

Funny, but she'd felt the same when she'd sat across from Reid in that conference room. Yes, they'd both gotten older, as evidenced by those tiny lines fanning out from the corners of Reid's eyes when he smiled. He'd finally grown into his lanky height too, his shoulders broadening and hard muscle filling in all his skinny limbs. Still, even with the changes, she sensed the old Reid — the kind, sweet, funny guy she'd known since childhood — lurking deep inside him. That was what made letting go so hard. She'd loved that guy, more than anything else.

The light turned green, and she accelerated. The farther she drove down this meandering road lining the coast, the more memories surfaced. The scenery was beautiful. Peaceful. Less hectic than the city. For a split second, she wondered what life would have been like had she stayed. Would she be a different person now?

Years ago, staying in Boulder Point hadn't been an option. There were no opportunities, and the slow, draining life of living paycheck to paycheck that she'd witnessed with her father would've slowly eaten away at Stacy until there was nothing left. Add in Gabby's torments and Reid's betrayal, and that pretty much sealed the deal for her.

No. She didn't regret leaving, and she was pretty

sure Reid didn't regret it either. He hadn't tried very hard to stop her from going. Nor had he attempted to contact her in the decade she'd been gone.

Her leaving hadn't devastated Reid. He was successful now with his own business. He'd moved on just fine without her.

Stacy lowered her window and inhaled the fresh sea air, the scent bringing with it happy childhood memories. The sparkling Atlantic beckoned, calming her frazzled nerves. The beach had always made her feel better. Would it still have that magical effect on her?

She drove to the inn, getting out of the car and staring out over the cliffs at the ocean. She'd almost forgotten about the private beach below. It had been one of her favorite places, secluded by two jetties that stretched out into the ocean on either side. Glancing to the left, she noticed the rickety stairs that led to the beach.

The steps were overgrown with bushes now and a lot more decrepit but looked as if they would work. The urge to go for a walk on the beach overwhelmed her. Later, though. First she needed to call her mother.

Ginny wasn't around, and she went to her room to make the call, her heart squeezing at the sadness in her mother's voice when she relayed the details about her father's luncheon.

"Thanks for taking care of that, honey," her mother said. "I'll pay you back when I get Dad's life insurance money."

"Don't be ridiculous. I'm not taking your money." Stacy had enough, and it was the least she could do. "What are you doing now? I was thinking we could take a walk on the beach."

"That's a lovely idea, but my bowling league is taking me out. Trying to cheer me up, I guess." Her mother's voice cracked, and then she sucked in a shaky breath. "But acting cheered up is half the battle. I'll take a rain check on that walk."

"Okay," Stacy said then asked, "Mom, how are you really doing?"

"Honestly, I'm okay. I miss your father, of course, but we had a great life, and I'm choosing to be grateful for that and not bitter that he's gone." Her mother paused. "I hope you got to reminisce a bit with Reid when you planned the luncheon."

"Umm, yeah, a bit." Stacy's concern for her mother had obliterated thoughts of Reid from her head, but now they were back. She didn't know if *reminisce* was the right word, but being with him had certainly brought back memories.

A car horn honked on the other end of the phone, and her mother said, "That's them. I better go. Thanks again."

Stacy tossed her phone on the bed, thoughts of Reid bubbling to the surface. He really had been her best friend, and they'd had so many good times. Truth was, she'd never connected with another man the way she had with him. But then all that shit had happened with Gabby and him not wanting to leave town.

And she'd suspected the worst.

Maybe she hadn't been fair. Maybe Brenda was right.

Her cheeks flamed as she remembered the nasty comment she'd made to Reid about him and Gabby drinking together earlier at the restaurant. Reid had looked upset, and she'd sensed sincerity in his explanation about how he'd just happened to be in the bar and didn't want her to drive drunk. That would be just like him to go out of his way to help someone.

She was ashamed at how she had acted earlier, practically calling him an adulterer and a liar. What was wrong with her?

She needed to stop acting as if she were in high school, but the feelings that bubbled up when she was around Reid confused her, and she ended up lashing out. She feared she might know the reason. Sure, those old wounds still stung, but seeing Reid today had brought up new feelings. Terrifying feelings. Feelings that made her worry that she wasn't completely over Reid Callahan.

Whoosh!

The window blew open and clattered against the wall, fluttering the curtain and letting in salty sea air and the sound of gulls.

The beach. Right. She should go walk on the beach. Combing the beach for shells and sea creatures had always been an activity that took her mind off her problems. And right now she had a big problem she needed to get off her mind.

She hurried to the stairs, picking her way through the overgrown shrubs and rose bushes. The steps, weatherworn gray and missing a few boards, remained sturdy enough. Finally at the bottom, she took off her shoes, walking barefoot onto the sunbaked sand.

Seagulls squawked in the air above, and near the horizon, a sailboat drifted lazily. Lulled into relaxation, Stacy walked closer to the water line and dipped in her toes. Brisk but refreshing. She rolled up her jeans and waded in a bit farther, ankle deep.

A few waves rolled toward her, and Stacy dodged them, laughing and frolicking like a kid again even though her toes were numb. She was blissfully alone.

The outcropping of rocks that stretched into the sea hid this tiny beach from the main beach and any curious onlookers.

Boulder Point had many beautiful beaches, but this one was her favorite. Good thing it was low tide, or she'd be completely swimming in seawater. It wouldn't be the first time she'd been caught there at high tide.

Memories continued to pull her under like a riptide. All the fun she and Brenda used to have here when they'd come with their parents, searching the tidal pools for starfish or crabs or snails. Later, in high school, she and Reid would sit on these rocks for hours, looking out over the water as they talked about their crappy home lives or Stacy getting bullied at school. After her father was laid off, a lot of her former wealthy friends distanced themselves from her.

She hadn't been one of the cool crowd anymore — with the best outfits and latest electronics. But Reid had stuck by her side through it all. He'd always been her best friend.

Until Gabby had become the major culprit in the bullying and things changed.

Stacy sighed and walked on a little farther, letting all her fears, all her hurt, float away, if only for a little while.

Mesmerized by the tiny universe within a tidal

pool before her, Stacy crouched to see the edge of a sand dollar sticking out. Carefully, she scraped the sand away, finding it intact — a rarity. Excitement built within her. This had to be a sign of better times to come, right?

Movement near the rocks drew her attention, and she looked up, her heart jerking in her chest when she saw Reid climbing over the top of the breakwater.

REID STOPPED short at the sight of the woman who'd been foremost in his mind since their meeting earlier. He'd come out here to clear his head, never expecting her to remember their special place, let alone show up.

He hadn't seen her car at the pull-off. He never would have come if he had. But here she was. Here *they* were. Ironic, because he'd been hoping the walk on the beach would take his mind off Stacy.

The sight of her brought a flood of memories. She stood barefoot in a tidal pool, her jeans rolled up and her long blond hair blowing around her face as if she'd never left, never changed from the sweet, carefree girl he'd once known.

He hesitated, not sure he was welcome. Not sure

he wanted to venture farther. "Uh, sorry. Didn't mean to intrude."

"It's fine," she said, holding her hand over her eyes to shield them from the sunshine. Reid wasn't so sure it was fine, but instead of turning around, he found himself walking toward her as if drawn by an invisible cord, stopping only to remove his boots and socks first.

"What's that?" He pointed at her hand.

Stacy held out her hand to reveal a perfectly formed sand dollar.

"Wow. I don't think I've seen one in such good condition since we were in school."

"Remember all those shells we found after the hurricane? How cool was that?" Stacy smiled, and his world brightened. Unlike the frosty demeanor she'd shown at the restaurant, Stacy seemed friendly. Almost like the *old* Stacy.

Every nerve screamed for him to run. Run before he fell under her spell again, only to be left in the dust. Run before he turned into a younger version of his father, puttering away, lonely, and pining for the only woman he ever loved who didn't think Boulder Point was good enough.

But he stayed.

"Very cool." Reid straightened, and they walked

farther along the shoreline. "I've been finding lots of good cobalt sea glass recently."

"Yeah?" She tucked her hair behind her ear. "You still come out here a lot?"

"Sure. I love it by the water. It's always been special to me."

To us.

He bit back the last words before they slipped out. She gave him some serious side-eye as they stopped near another outcropping of rocks.

"How long will you be in town?" he asked before he could stop himself.

"Only until Saturday." Stacy crossed her arms, her T-shirt billowing in the warm early-summer breeze. "Mom and Brenda need help sorting through all Dad's stuff, and there's estate paperwork to handle. I'm hoping to get a jump on it after the service tomorrow."

"Then it's back to the big city, huh?" Unexpected sadness pinched his chest.

"Yeah. Back to Columbus." She looked around, her expression turning wistful. "I didn't realize how much I missed all of this."

"Yeah." They were a good distance now from where they started. Reid bent and turned up a rock, revealing a starfish underneath.

A tiny hermit crab emerged from the sand nearby,

and Stacy laughed, picking it up and holding it in her palm. The little creature snapped its pincher claw at her in outrage. "I almost wish now I'd taken more time off work."

She put the tiny crab back on the sand and watched it scuttle away.

"Remember when we used to come here as kids?" he asked, remembering happier times. "We'd sit out on the rocks for hours, watching all that puffy seaweed tangle around the shore?"

"I do," she said, meeting his gaze. In her eyes, he saw sadness and regret and a hint of affection. That last emotion ignited a flicker of hope inside him — hope that maybe the girl he'd lost so long ago wasn't entirely beyond his reach.

A large wave crashed on shore, sending a spray of cold water toward them. Giggling and screaming, they both raced for the nearby boulders, scrambling atop to avoid the worst of it. Reid took Stacy's arm to steady her. They were close enough now for her heat to penetrate his clothes, close enough for her sweet lily scent to fill his head with all sorts of dangerous ideas. Close enough for all his long-buried emotions to rush back in a dangerous torrent of need.

Their gazes locked. His pulse pounded loudly in his ears as she turned to face him, her palm resting against his chest, right over his heart. Time seemed to slow, and Reid couldn't help wondering if she still tasted like strawberries and cream.

Their lips drew closer, closer ...

A horn honked from the roadway above.

Startled, Stacy stepped away from him, giving a nervous laugh and clearing her throat. "Guess, uh, I'm not used to climbing these rocks anymore. I almost lost my balance."

"Yeah. Me too." He raked a hand through his hair and frowned. Somewhere between taking a break at the restaurant and finding her on the beach, he'd lost complete control of the situation. "I, uh, I should get back to work." He jumped down from the rock then reached up to help her, feeling discombobulated. "Lots to do before tomorrow."

"Right." Stacy looked as stunned as he felt. She jumped down unaided and headed toward the stairs that led to the inn. Reid had almost forgotten about those. That explained why he hadn't seen her car. "I need to go too. See you tomorrow."

He watched her climb the steps, whispering to himself, "See you around, Stacy."

Reid stood there, alone, his jumbled feelings racing between relief and panic.

He had a good life that he loved here in Boulder

Point. Things had finally settled into place, and he wasn't ready to jostle all that for a woman who might get bored and leave. Was he?

This town hadn't been enough for Stacy. *He* hadn't been enough. Forget about the whole argument they'd had over Gabby — the real truth was that he hadn't been important enough to Stacy to make her stay.

He'd wanted to beg her, to promise her anything, but in the end, he'd remained silent. He didn't want to hold her back. Didn't want to be the reason she looked back on her life in disappointment, never knowing if she could have made something of herself.

And after she'd left, he'd been so broken he hadn't even been able to pick up the phone to call her.

Ten years had gone by, and his feelings for her hadn't dimmed. But now things were a bit different. Stacy had already proved that she could make something of herself. Now that she'd done that, would she consider moving back?

She'd made it clear she was staying only for the week, but the look on her face when she'd stared at the ocean read downright homesick.

For a crazy second, Reid wondered if she might consider staying, starting over here, giving Boulder Point another chance. Giving *them* another chance.

CHAPTER 8

After her unexpected beach encounter with Reid, Stacy rushed back to the Firefly Inn. Things had seemed so right, so normal with him, that she'd nearly lost herself in the moment and kissed him.

She shook her head as she walked up the front steps. Thank goodness her common sense — and no small amount of fear — had interceded. Kissing Reid Callahan would've been a monumental mistake. Nothing could ever work out between them, not with all the issues of the past. So why was she even considering it?

It made no sense.

Besides, even if she decided to stick around town, there was Gabby to contend with and the not-so-small matter of what she'd do for a living. There wasn't a large hotel within one hundred miles. No way could Stacy support herself as an event planner.

Nope. It was stupid to even entertain the idea of moving back to Boulder Point.

It was crazy, ludicrous, insane.

She headed inside, deep in thought.

"Everything okay?" Ginny called out as Stacy passed the old library.

She stopped and backed up to peek through the door. Ginny sat in the center of the room, her expression harried, blueprints, pens, and markers scattered on the table before her. Stacy forced a smile. "Fine. I finished finalizing the arrangements for my dad's memorial luncheon earlier and just came up from the beach."

"The beach is wonderful, isn't it?" Ginny said. "Until I moved to town, I never knew how amazing the Atlantic Ocean was. Donald and I visited, of course, when we considered buying this property, but we were too busy discussing finances to pay much attention." She sighed and glanced over her shoulder and out the windows. "I'm glad now that we didn't make memories here. This way, there aren't any fond remembrances of my husband to make me sad."

The sorrow in Ginny's voice pinched Stacy's

chest. If she'd stayed here, she could've ended up like Ginny. Or her mother.

The thought made her heart ache worse. She'd only seen her mother right after flying in and talked to her on the phone earlier. Stacy understood her mother trying to keep busy to keep her mind off things, but she wanted to spend more time with her. Being back in Boulder Point made her long for the closeness of family.

Stacy stepped closer to the table and glanced down at Ginny's paperwork. They were plans for some sort of event, with seating arrangements and catering menus. Familiar territory. She pointed to a sheet and smiled. "Plans for your first event?"

"Yep." Ginny gestured for her to take a seat at the table. "These are for the big wedding next month. Donald and I used to host things like this at some of our other properties, but he usually handled most of the details while I played hostess on the big day. I'm feeling a bit out of my element now, unfortunately. This wedding could bring in a lot of new business for the inn if it's successful, but I'm afraid I might be in over my head."

Stacy felt for Ginny. She wanted her business to be successful, and she'd planned dozens of events much more complicated than a wedding. "Maybe I can help."

Ginny looked up at her. "Oh, I wouldn't want to impose on you, especially with your father's services and all."

"No problem. This is what I do for a living." Stacy picked up the nearest spreadsheet listing party supplies, noticing several areas where she could cut both costs and time for Ginny. "And it's a nice distraction from the sadness, so I'm happy to help."

They spent the next hour going over everything from the best use of the gardens for the ceremony to table arrangements for the reception and placement of the arbors and dance floor. She even assisted Ginny with tweaking a catering menu to appeal to both vegans and gluten-free guests.

"Wow," Ginny said once they were finished. "You're really great at this. Too bad you're leaving soon. I could use someone like you on my team."

"Are you offering me a job?" Stacy laughed, standing and stretching.

"Are you looking for one?" Ginny countered, not laughing.

"No, I'm not. But thank you for thinking of me. Now, if you'll excuse me, I need to run up to my room for a minute."

"Of course." Ginny nodded, her expression now glowing with excitement. "Thanks again, Stacy. I can't wait to get started on this event."

As she climbed the stairs, Stacy couldn't help grinning to herself. It felt good to help someone in true need, even better and more rewarding than her job back home. In Columbus, she worked mainly on large, lavish events with big corporations or uber-wealthy clients. Rarely did any of them thank her in person. Her bosses were always appreciative of her efforts, but working with Ginny felt different.

Her cell phone rang as she stepped back into her room. Maybe it was her mother wanting to take that beach walk. But Brenda's name popped up on the caller ID as she answered. "Hey, sis. What's up?"

"How'd the meeting with Reid go?" Brenda asked.

"Fine. Everything's set for tomorrow." Stacy had no intention of sharing their interlude on the beach afterward. "It's all taken care of."

"Perfect. Hey, I wanted to invite you for dinner tonight," Brenda said. "Tommy's got the night off, so he can watch Sammy."

"Sure. Sounds great. Afterward, maybe we can have girl time and talk like we used to when we were kids. Is Mom coming?"

"Perfect." Brenda's warm tone felt like a hug. "I

think Mom's pretty busy today. She mentioned something about going out with her friends again tonight."

"Oh." Stacy did her best to hide her disappointment. After all, it was good her mother wasn't sitting at
home, mired in grief. "Okay."

"I've got a couple of errands to run, so I'll swing by
the inn and pick you up about six?" Brenda said. "And
this time it's my treat."

"We'll argue over the bill once we get there. It's
tradition," Stacy said. "See you later."

She ended the call then flopped down on her bed.
Her sister shouldn't pay tonight. Brenda and Tommy
struggled to keep their heads above financial waters.
Work at the mill was sparse these days, and her sister
was a stay-at-home mom. Sammy wasn't in school yet,
but once he got older, expenses would only continue to
increase.

Besides, Stacy made good money and had no one
to spend it on. While she was in Boulder Point, her
family wouldn't pay for anything, she decided. And
yeah, they'd still argue about the bill because that was
what they did, but Stacy would make sure she won in
the end.

She rolled over and looked at the clock on the
nightstand. It was only a bit after noon. She had hours

before Brenda was due to pick her up. Yawning, Stacy shut off her phone, plugging it into its charger before rolling over and taking a much-needed nap.

She woke several hours later, refreshed and ready for dinner. After a shower and a change of clothes, Stacy finished applying her makeup and doing her hair then headed downstairs to wait for her sister. The delicious smells of Yankee pot roast and roasted potatoes greeted her, and her heart sank. She should've said something to Ginny earlier. If Maisie had prepared a full dinner, as she'd done for breakfast, it would be a waste.

"Don't you look nice," Ginny said, meeting her at the bottom of the stairs. Stacy had dressed in black pants and a slim short-sleeved black sweater with tiny red hearts embroidered all over it. "Plans tonight?"

"Yes. My sister Brenda's picking me up for dinner at six. I'm so sorry I didn't say something to you before." Stacy sniffed the yummy-scented air, and her stomach growled. "I know I'm your only guest, so I hope that doesn't put you out."

"No, no, dear. It's fine. Maisie's only cooking for the two of us this evening. If we have extra, we bring it to the homeless shelter. Besides, you need to spend time with your family. That's why you're here, to reconnect and support each other during this difficult time. Like I said before, family is important, and you never know when you'll get another chance to see them, especially with you living so far away. Once you leave for Ohio again, it'll be too late, so see them as much as you can now."

"Thanks." Ginny was right, as always. Seemed the older woman had an uncanny ability to get right to the heart of the matter and reveal the truth of a situation, sometimes when Stacy couldn't even see it herself. "I'll just wait in the parlor for Brenda, if that's okay."

"Absolutely, dear. You have a wonderful time this evening. You deserve it." Ginny gave a small wave then disappeared down the hall toward the kitchen.

Stacy walked outside and took a seat on a lovely Victorian-style settee near the front windows. If she were honest, spending time with Reid earlier had left her unsettled and lonely. Seeing him again had opened a door that she'd forgotten existed.

Now, all her memories of this town, these people, her family, rushed over her, leaving her flayed and vulnerable. She only wished their mother could join her and Brenda tonight, but she wouldn't think of disrupting her plans. The poor thing had been through enough already. No need to create more chaos.

Besides, they'd spend lots of time together at the funeral tomorrow.

Tonight would be about her and Brenda reconnecting. After all, with Dad gone, there were fewer Brightons left in the world. Time to treasure those closest to her and make sure they didn't drift any further apart.

CHAPTER 9

Brenda picked Stacy up promptly at six. She climbed into the passenger seat of her sister's minivan, moving aside an empty juice box and several toys before buckling her seat belt.

Once settled, Stacy smiled at Brenda, who looked as cute as always in her faded jeans and pink sweater. "Hey. Thanks for coming to get me. This was a great idea."

"No problem." Brenda signaled then pulled out into traffic. "Any preference for where we eat?"

"Nope. I don't even know what's good here anymore. You decide."

"Awesome." Her sister made a left and drove around the block to head back in the opposite direction. "I know just the place."

They pulled into the lot of a sleek, upscale-looking bistro, quite chic for little Boulder Point. They got out of the van, and Stacy straightened her black pants and sweater. "Do I look okay to go in here?"

"You look gorgeous, as always, sis." Brenda gestured toward her own casual outfit. "Trust me. The food's fancy, but not the atmosphere."

Inside, it was quite lovely. Dark carpeting, dim lighting, candles flickering on the white-linen-covered tables. The restaurant sat near the wharf, and the far wall was all glass, looking out over the marina, where several moored boats swayed. Fishing trawlers puttered past, their lights glimmering merrily in the gathering twilight. The fresh smell of sea air mixed with the savory aroma of grilled meat.

Stacy remembered coming down to the wharf with her father for work. He'd always loved the water too, just like Reid. Fresh sorrow pinched her chest for both of the men she'd lost.

"This place is really nice." Stacy walked over to look at a line of black-and-white photos lining the wall of the waiting area. Many featured local fishermen with their catches of the day. The last one was the mayor of Boulder Point and ... Stacy glanced back at Brenda over her shoulder. "Who owns this restaurant?"

"Reid Callahan. Didn't I tell you?" Brenda said, her smile innocent.

"No. You didn't. Did you?" Stacy straightened. Brenda *had* mentioned the name of his restaurant the other night, but Stacy hadn't paid much attention and didn't connect the dots when they'd driven into the parking lot. Her heart thudded nervously at the thought of seeing Reid again, but she couldn't very well run out of the restaurant. Funny that Brenda would pick this very restaurant. It was nice, but Stacy doubted it was the only suitable option in the area.

Her gaze narrowed at Brenda. Just what was her sister up to?

She had to admit Reid had done all right for himself. The place was packed, even this early. Seemed Reid had come a long way from the one lobster boat he'd owned when Stacy lived in town. The hostess led them to a table for two near the window. She filled their water goblets and handed them menus before leaving them to decide. "It really is beautiful here."

"See what you're missing in Ohio, sis?" Brenda gave her a look over the top of her menu. "Sure you don't want to move back?"

"I'm happy where I'm at, thanks." Stacy sipped her water. And she was happy in Columbus, though she had to admit that lately she'd started to wonder if there was more to the world than her corporate rat race, more than the next big client, the next big event. "But nothing beats these views."

"True." Brenda smiled as the waitress arrived, and they placed their orders — a rib-eye steak for Brenda, shrimp scampi for Stacy. "And two glasses of white wine," her sister said, giving Stacy a wink. "We deserve it."

The waitress grinned and headed for the bar to get their drinks while Stacy took a longer look around the restaurant. Perhaps she'd luck out and Reid wouldn't even be here this evening. Bad enough that, each time she closed her eyes, she still pictured him on the beach, so close she felt his heat through her clothes, smelled his clean musky scent, the fragrance warming her from the inside out.

Stacy blinked hard against the memories and stared into the shadows across the room.

As if conjured by her thoughts, Reid emerged from a doorway behind the bar. He'd changed since this afternoon, now wearing a black T-shirt and blazer, his thick dark hair gleaming beneath the overhead lights and his smile wide and bright. Before she could look away, their eyes met, and her stomach flipped. She saw surprise and no small amount of hesitation race through his gaze. Nervous butterflies took flight in her bloodstream.

To her eternal gratitude, he headed in the opposite direction, greeting guests and chatting with them, giving Stacy ample time to admire his graceful moves and easy, accommodating air. All too soon, however, he made his way toward their table.

"Good evening, ladies," he said, giving Brenda a friendly grin before shifting his attention to Stacy. His smile took on a slight edge, and heat sparked in his stormy gray eyes. "Glad to see you at The Mariner this evening. Everything good so far?"

"Everything's lovely, as always," Brenda said, patting his forearm. "I figured I'd show my sister the nicer side of Boulder Point since she's been out of touch for so long."

"Yes. Must be hard for you, leaving all the hustle and bustle of the city behind," Reid said, his deep voice sliding over Stacy like a caress. "Though it was good to see you again today."

Thankfully he provided no details of their beach rendezvous. Her sister would've been all over that like barracuda on bait.

"You too," Stacy managed to croak out of her dry throat. She took another sip of water and met her sister's I-told-you-so look with a mind-your-own-business stare. "Looks like you have another winning business on your hands here. Congratulations."

The waitress brought their wine then quickly departed for another table.

"Thanks. It's been a lot of hard work and perseverance, but worth it in the end." He narrowed his gaze. "I'm sure you've worked hard to get where you're at in your career. What's the name of the company you work for again?"

"Bryce Wallace Associates." Stacy frowned, realizing she'd not checked her emails once today. In fact, even the company name sounded a million miles away now. "They're one of the top fifteen event-planning firms in the nation."

"That's great," Reid said, one side of his full lips quirking up in a sad little smile. "I always knew you were destined for greatness."

"Yeah," she said, her voice going all breathy without her consent. "You too."

Brenda watched them both in amused silence, sipping her wine.

Reid opened his mouth as if to say more, but a loud crash sounded from the kitchen. He frowned over his shoulder then stepped away from their table. "I'd better check that out. Enjoy your meals, ladies."

He took off across the restaurant, and Stacy watched him go, loneliness tightening her stomach.

"Don't worry, sis. He'll be back, I'm sure." Brenda said. "Maybe he's another reason you'd want to stick around, eh?"

"What?" Stacy frowned at her sibling. "No. Reid has his hands full with his businesses. Besides, I'm here for you and Mom. This is about us, about family. You never know when you'll get another chance to be with those you love, and I don't want to miss my opportunity."

"Hmm." Brenda pulled her ringing phone from her purse and scowled at the screen. "I'm sorry, sis, but it's Tommy. Sammy hasn't been feeling well today, so I need to take this."

"No problem." Stacy nodded as Brenda walked back to the lobby area for privacy.

"Here're some rolls for you to enjoy," the waitress said, dropping off a wire basket covered in linen. "Your salads should be out shortly."

"Thanks." Stacy snatched one of the still-warm-from-the-oven cheddar biscuits and bit into it. The roll was delightfully crispy on the outside and soft inside. She slathered fresh butter onto it and popped another bite in her mouth. Heaven — that was what it was.

Sweet and salty and practically melting in her mouth it was so fluffy.

"Good?" Reid's smooth tone had her eyes snapping open.

She'd been so wrapped up in her food-gasm she hadn't even heard him return. He watched with a small knowing smile.

Brenda rushed back to the table. "Hey, sis. I'm so sorry, but I need to go. Tommy's got a ... *situation* ... and it requires mom intervention." She grabbed her purse before turning to Reid. "Can you give Stacy a ride back to the inn?"

"Uh, sure." Reid stepped aside as the waitress brought their salads. "What about your dinner? I'd hate to see that rib eye go to waste."

Brenda's gaze darted between the two of them, and Stacy's suspicions grew. Maybe there wasn't a situation at all. Maybe her sister was just trying to find another excuse to force her and Reid together.

"It's fine," Stacy said, standing. "I can wait for them to pack up dinner and then find my own way back to the inn. No need to trouble anyone. Is Sammy okay?"

"Sammy's fine. Just super fussy with the croup," Brenda said. "And don't be silly. Stay and enjoy your dinner, sis. Maybe Reid can take a break and join you so you don't have to eat alone." She all but forced the guy into her vacant seat across the table from Stacy. "Enjoy. See you both tomorrow."

With that, Brenda rushed out, leaving Stacy to stare after her. Cheeks heated, she hazarded a glance at Reid, finding him looking as gobsmacked as she felt. Slowly, Stacy sank back into her seat and forced a smile. "So, I guess we're sharing a meal then, huh?"

REID STARED across the candlelit table at Stacy, his heart in his throat. He was the owner of the restaurant. He should get up and get back to work. He should walk around, greeting his guests, schmoozing with the clientele.

He stayed put.

Stacy looked even more appealing tonight, if that were possible. The soft glow of the flame highlighted that adorable smattering of freckles across her nose and cheeks and caught the glint of copper in her hair. She gave a lopsided, somewhat embarrassed smile, which revealed that one little dimple in her right cheek. The one that made his heart pound and his toes curl in his leather loafers.

He'd dated plenty in the years since she'd left and

had his share of affairs, but no one had ever affected him like Stacy Brighton. Reid had fooled himself into thinking there was something better out there — a brighter, stronger, more passionate love. But now, sitting across from her tonight, he knew it wasn't true.

She focused on fixing her salad, not meeting his gaze. "So."

"Yeah." He poured ranch dressing on his greens then picked up his fork. "Looks like we're having dinner. I hate to waste food."

"Me too." She sounded tentative as she nibbled on her vegetables. "Sorry I, um, rushed off at the beach earlier today. With all that's happened with my father and coming here, it's thrown me a bit off-kilter."

"No, no." He swallowed a bite of lettuce, happy to find the greens crisp and sharp, and the homemade peppercorn ranch creamy and delicious. He'd have to thank his staff later. Of course, his lovely dinner partner didn't hurt. "No apologies necessary. You've got so much on your plate right now. It's perfectly understandable."

They ate in silence for a while until Reid couldn't stand it any longer. He swallowed his last bite of salad and then pushed his plate away. The longer he sat, the more he noticed the aura of tragedy surrounding Stacy. As crazy as it seemed, he longed to bring back the smiling, carefree woman from the beach earlier, if only for a little while. After the waitress came and cleared his empty plate, he sat forward and smiled. "So, event planning, huh?"

"Yes." She dabbed her mouth with her napkin and then sipped her wine. "It keeps me busy."

"I'll bet." Finally, they had some common ground. "The events I handle around here, plus the daily grind of the restaurants, always keeps me on my toes."

"Do people host a lot of events?" Stacy smiled at the server who took her empty salad plate. "When I drove through town earlier, I saw some shops boarded up and homes for sale. Looks like the economy here was hit hard."

"Yeah, things were rough for a while, but they're rebounding finally. The last few years, the Boulder Point Town Council has really focused on bringing in more tourism dollars. And my catering company does a lot of advertising in some of the larger cities in the area to draw business. Summer is by far our busiest time, with all the weddings and family reunions."

"And the occasional memorial service," Stacy said, looking at him as the server placed their entrees on the table. "Thanks again for agreeing to handle my father's luncheon."

"No problem. Happy to do it." Reid requested

drink refills for both of them before digging into his rib-eye steak. Juicy, perfectly cooked, and the russet herbed smashed potatoes on the side were the perfect complement. He'd give Bruce his compliments later.

Stacy seemed to enjoy her shrimp scampi, if her groans of pleasure were any indication. He cleared his throat and swallowed hard against the sudden lump in his throat. "Your dad was a good man. John fell on hard times, but he still stuck around to care for his family. That's way more than I can say for my mom."

"Have you heard from her at all?" Stacy asked, sipping her water.

"Nothing. Not sure I'd even want to anymore." He stared out the window at the harbor beyond. Sitting here, talking to Stacy, felt good. Like old times. He hadn't realized until now how much he'd missed her. "She's part of my past. A part I put behind me a long time ago. Got to move on and keep going, you know?"

"Yeah, I know." She gave him a sad smile and focused on her food once more.

By the time they were finished, he felt full and content for the first time in years.

The waitress returned to check on them and remove their dishes. "Would either of you care for dessert? We have a wonderful turtle cheesecake, made fresh today by our chef."

"Oh." Stacy met his gaze across the table. If he remembered correctly, she'd always been a sucker for chocolate and graham crackers. "That sounds delicious."

"We'll take a slice, Mindy," Reid said to the waitress. "Two forks. And coffees, please."

"Coming right up, sir." The server grinned and gave him a slight bow before hurrying back to the kitchen. She returned a moment later with white mugs of steaming brew and their cheesecake.

"So what's new in Boulder Point?" Stacy asked, stirring cream and sugar into her cup. "I thought I saw a couple of new fast-food places on my way in from the airport."

"Yeah. They're adding a Starbucks near the courthouse in a couple of months."

"Wow. You guys are coming up in the world."

"This place has always been pretty perfect to me."

She gave him a fond look. "Yes. I remember you used to love working down at the docks, pulling in lobster traps."

"Still do. I volunteer on the trawlers at least once or twice a month. There's something about using my hands, really getting into it." He flexed his fingers and didn't miss the way her gaze tracked the tiny movement. Suddenly, the tone of their conversation shifted toward the more personal again. "It was nice. Being with you on the beach today. Made me recall how close we were once upon a time."

"Yeah." She tucked a blond curl behind her ear, and he fought the crazy urge to slide his fingers through her hair to see if it felt as soft and silky as he remembered. "Like I said, I'm sorry I had to rush away when I did," she continued. "Things are difficult right now."

"Want to take a walk after we're done with dinner?" Reid asked, handing her a dessert fork. He'd not meant to ask that out loud. But now that the offer was on the table, he couldn't say he regretted it.

"Oh, I'm not really dressed for beach walking tonight, I'm afraid." She stuck out her leg so he could see her spike-heeled pumps, the same expensive ones she'd been wearing the day of their accident. "Maybe another time."

"How about the docks, then?" He carved off a bite of cheesecake and popped it into his mouth, savoring the rich chocolate and creamy cheese, the gooey, salty caramel, and crisp graham cracker crust. More kudos to Bruce. "C'mon. It'll help you burn off some of the calories from this dessert. Not that you need to. You look just fine from where I'm sitting."

Reid gave himself a mental smackdown. *Way to act creepy, dude.*

Pink color rose in Stacy's cheeks, making her even lovelier in the candlelight. She gave him a small smile and took a tiny bite of the decadent dessert. Another quiet moan issued from her parted lips and jolted through his system like pure lightning.

Finally, she exhaled and gave a small shrug. "Okay. I guess a short walk couldn't hurt. It'll be nice to get some air, anyway, since I'll be inside most of the day tomorrow at the funeral home."

He refrained from grinning, given the solemn nature of her last statement, but still fist-pumped inside his head over the small victory. They finished the dessert quickly, along with their coffee, then headed outside to his truck. The docks were only a few blocks away, but he didn't want to risk her tiring out or changing her mind between here and there.

A tingle of excitement shot through Reid as he helped Stacy into her seat before he went around to his side and climbed behind the wheel. He'd not felt that burst of internal fireworks since high school. This felt good, right. He wanted more. They drove in silence to the small parking lot adjacent to the wharf, where he got out first to hold the door for Stacy. The gentle lap of waves against the docks and the cries of the seagulls gave him a sense of home and belonging, and the tang of salt and fish in the air made him smile.

"This area hasn't changed much at all," she said as she waited for him to lock the truck. Boulder Point knew where its main source of income was, and the town fathers invested well in keeping up the harbor and the neighboring property.

The town council had even dedicated money to keeping up a boardwalk around the area for the tourists. He and Stacy strolled there now, enjoying the cool breeze and the full moon's light. Stars twinkled in the sky above. Reid couldn't remember a more gorgeous night.

"Do you ever miss this town?" he asked. At least he'd stopped himself from asking if she ever missed him, fearing he already knew the answer. "You've got a lot of memories here."

She shrugged, gave a sad little sniff. "Usually I'm too busy to think about anything except work. But now that I'm here, it brings back a lot of stuff."

They stopped near the end of the dock to peer out across the black expanse of the Atlantic. Reid wanted to ask her exactly what kind of "stuff" she meant, but refrained. Her expression was rapt, enchanted, and that spark of hope flared inside him again. That wasn't the look of someone who couldn't wait to leave town.

That was the look of someone who missed what they'd left behind, and maybe, just maybe, wanted to get it back.

As they returned to his truck, he decided to plant a tiny seed in her head, hoping it might grow in the days he had left with her. "You know, the housing market here is great right now. Lots of oceanfront views for rock-bottom prices. Won't last long, though, with all the tourists flooding into the place each year. They're snapping them up like hotcakes."

"Really?" She said, clicking her seat belt into place. "That's great for the locals. Drives up property values for everyone else, right?"

"Right." He started the engine and frowned. Not the point he was trying to make, but he still had a few days to make her see how much she missed Boulder Point and how much she belonged here. After her father's services tomorrow, Reid planned to start showing Stacy just how exciting, inviting, and desirable moving back to Maine and coastal living could be.

"Let's get you back to the inn," he said, pulling out of the lot. "You've got a long day tomorrow, and I've got food to prepare and gear to load in the catering trucks."

CHAPTER 10

"Well, here we are," Reid announced.

He had pulled up outside the Firefly Inn, and Stacy sat staring out the window at the lovely old home. The whole evening had felt like a trip to a more pleasant time. Even the route Reid had taken to get her back to the inn had been the same one they'd traveled many times as teens.

She cleared her throat and unbuckled her seat belt slowly, suddenly loath to see the evening end and unsure how to handle those feelings. "Thank you for the ride. I appreciate it."

"No problem." Reid cut the engine and opened his door, smiling at her inquiring look. "What kind of gentleman would I be if I didn't walk a lady to her door? My dad would never forgive me."

A fresh wave of butterflies took flight in Stacy's

stomach. He was simply being polite, she kept telling herself. Yet with the full moon's light bouncing off the ocean waves in the distance and the sweet scent of honeysuckle and sea salt mingling in the air, there was a hint of magic.

With Reid's assistance, she got out of the truck, the touch of his hand on hers lighting her up inside like one of the countless fireflies glowing in the field nearby.

They took their time heading up to the inn's wraparound porch, lingering to watch the breeze ripple over the meadow beside the property.

"Remember when we used to catch those lightning bugs?" Reid asked.

"Yeah." Stacy gave a fond grin. "We always used to tell stories about how this place was haunted. I'm glad someone took it on and gave it new life."

"Ginny's worked super hard to get it back into condition." Reid stopped and took a deep breath, gazing out over the cliffs in the distance. "Can you hear the waves?"

"I can." She breathed deeply of the fresh ocean air. "Ginny asked me to help her with a wedding next month here at the inn. You might want to talk to her too. She'll need someone to take over once I'm gone."

He gave an exaggerated shudder and peeked one

eye open at her. "I don't know. With all the ghosts and stuff lurking about, I'm not sure I'm brave enough to venture inside."

"Seriously?" Stacy laughed. "Ginny said she found a bunch of old stuff inside the house. Furniture, photos, even a whole collection of salt and pepper shakers."

"Bet some of that's worth some money."

"Probably. I remember us sneaking in there. It was in bad shape at that time. Old dust covers on all the furniture, worn and water-stained wallpaper, sagging ceilings. I was afraid to go inside, but once we were in there, it felt almost ... *homey*."

"Homey?" Reid squinted at her.

"I know, it sounds weird." Stacy chuckled. "But it feels like the house is welcoming us now." She didn't mention the phantom figure she'd thought she'd seen in the library yesterday or the voice she'd heard on the stairs the first day. Reid had enough misgivings about the inn. She didn't want to add to them. Besides, she wasn't sure if she'd simply imagined them. "Well, thanks again for having dinner with me. I do wish you would let me pay for it, though."

He scoffed. "Don't be silly. I own the place. It's one of the perks."

They stood on the stairs leading up to the porch,

Stacy one step higher than Reid, putting them almost at eye level. He held on to the railing and inched nearer.

Those butterflies swarming inside her rioted.

"But next time we go out, you can pay," he said, his voice lower and his gaze flickering to her lips before returning to her eyes.

Stacy swallowed hard against the tightness in her throat. "Next time?"

Reid nodded, slipping his index finger beneath her chin and tilting her face up to his. The heat in his eyes felt familiar and fascinatingly new, all at the same time. The last time they'd stood this close, they'd been teenagers.

Now, they were both adults, with responsibilities and expectations and ...

His soft lips brushed hers, once, twice, before capturing them in a sweet kiss. Stacy held her breath, until her heart decided for her and she slid her arms around his neck to pull him closer, her lips opening beneath his to deepen the kiss.

REID TIGHTENED his hold on Stacy, pulling her closer, afraid if he broke contact for even a second, she'd disappear as fast as she had on the beach earlier. Her lips were just as soft, the taste of her just as sweet, as he remembered. A soft mewling sound came from her, and his heart melted. Until that moment, he hadn't realized how long he'd waited to have her in his arms again, how much he'd missed having her by his side.

If the way she clung to him was any indication, she might be feeling the same way.

Then, as quickly as the kiss started, it ended.

Stacy placed her palm against his chest and pushed gently, moving him back, away from her. For a moment, all he could do was blink down at her mouth, still dazed and lost in the blissful haze of awareness. Her eyes had a dreamy look in them, as if she couldn't quite believe what had just happened but wanted very much for it to happen again. He started to reach for her, but she frowned and shook her head.

Reid let his arms drop to his sides. She was right. Pushing things between them now wasn't smart. With her father's funeral the next day, she had far too much on her mind already. He stepped down off the stairs to the sidewalk and ran a shaky hand through his hair. "Sorry about that. I'm not sure what came over me."

"No, no," she said, her cheeks flushing a delightful shade of pink. "It's okay."

She bit her bottom lip, still swollen from his kisses.

To keep from touching her again, he shoved his hands in his pockets and rocked back on his heels.

"I should probably get inside," Stacy said, staring down at her toes. "Busy day tomorrow and all ..."

"Yep." He jammed the toe of his shoe into the concrete, feeling every bit as awkward as he had when he'd been a teenager. Stacy was still the most beautiful woman he'd ever met, and even now, all these years later, she still made him feel like a rookie in the love department. "Don't worry about the memorial lunch. I've got everything under control. Is there anything else you need?"

"Oh, no. Thanks for the offer, though." She sighed and stared out over the ocean. "Honestly, I'm not sure what I need at this point. My top priority is getting through the day tomorrow. Then I guess I'll take it from there."

He nodded, watching as she opened the inn's big oak door and went inside. He stood there for a few minutes after she'd gone, just thinking about things. Part of him was hopeful that perhaps things between them might work out after all. After all, they'd shared a good night together and the sweetest kiss in his recent memory.

The other part of him, though, was terrified.

This terror urged him back to his truck and out

onto the road, down the main drag of town and out to his favorite spot on the beach — the same spot where he and Stacy had met earlier. He climbed back to the rocks and sat, gazing out over the water, the salty breeze ruffling his hair and soothing his anxieties.

His fears came from the fact that, after tomorrow, he'd have only a few days left to convince Stacy that Boulder Point, Maine, wasn't the same dead-end place she'd left a decade ago. That the town, and he, had evolved, grown, and now offered all sorts of wonderful opportunities, if only she'd accept them.

There was one thing that could mess it up: Gabby. Reid knew that old argument might surface, and he wouldn't have any better answers than he'd had ten years ago. Chances were slim to none he could convince Gabby to let him share her secret, but if it meant getting Stacy back, he'd try.

And if his plans failed, well then, he'd return to his life and she'd return to Ohio, and he'd have to find a way to make peace with that.

A white gull swooped nearby and shifted his attention.

Of course, there was always a chance that his plan would work. That Gabby would see the light, would see that times had changed and she had nothing to feel guilty or ashamed about, except for the way she'd treated Stacy when they'd been in school. That would require an apology.

Then if things did go his way, he'd have a different set of issues to deal with — how to fit Stacy into his new life, how to help her get settled, and how to keep her close. He had a feeling he wouldn't mind *those* issues, not one bit.

She'd mentioned helping Ginny with event planning at the inn, and that was an excellent start. Her family was here, and he knew she wanted to be closer to them. And she clearly missed the ocean. All he had to do was play his cards right and make the most of the next few days to convince Stacy everything she needed, including Reid, was right here in Boulder Point.

CHAPTER 11

Stacy arrived at the funeral home half an hour earlier than necessary, hoping for a chance to center herself before the crowds arrived. When she pulled into the lot, she saw her sister's van parked near the entrance. Brenda and Tommy were in the foyer, doing their best to keep young Sammy occupied.

"Hey," Stacy said, giving her sister a hug. "How are you holding up?"

"Fine." Brenda sniffled slightly and gave Stacy a watery smile. "Better once all this is over."

"Yeah, I know." She turned to Tommy next. She'd always liked her brother-in-law and gave him a hug before kneeling in front of Sammy. "Hi there, mister."

The kid looked cute in his tiny suit, smiling and laughing despite the sadness of the day. If only everyone could stay inside such a happy bubble forever. Her heart broke a bit knowing the innocence wouldn't last. At first he gave Stacy a wary look, not having seen her for quite a while. Then, slowly, his smile returned, showing that adorable dimple in his right cheek, the same as Stacy's. Still, he clung to his mother's long black skirt, playing peek-a-boo with Stacy until he was sure she was all right.

"C'mon, Sammy," Brenda said, running her fingers through his silky blond hair. "You remember your Aunt Stace, right?"

Tommy crouched on the boy's other side, the resemblance between father and son unmistakable. The loving bond between them was evident, constricting Stacy's chest. Her father was gone. She'd never felt so isolated.

Sammy peeked out at Stacy again, and she forced herself to smile.

"Can you say hi?" Tommy asked him.

Sammy nodded then stepped out from behind Brenda's skirt, tentatively holding up his little arms. "Aunt Stace!"

Shocked for a second, Stacy stared wide-eyed at her nephew. Then she scooped him up and twirled him around as he giggled. She'd always wanted children someday, always expected she'd have some. The pull now felt stronger than ever.

Sure, she was still young, but something about holding Sammy close, feeling the fluff of his hair against her cheek, smelling the clean toddler smell of his skin as he cuddled warm and soft against her neck, made her melt. The tightness in her chest eased under his hug, and for the first time since she'd come home, Stacy felt as if her burden of grief and regret had lifted and she could breathe at last.

"Ah-hem." The funeral director stood at the top of the nearby stairs and cleared his throat. "Sorry to interrupt, folks, but it's time to get started."

Stacy put Sammy down and took his hand, following her sister and brother-in-law into the reception room, where her father's casket rested on a black-satin-covered platform at the front of the room.

Soft instrumental music drifted into the space through the overhead speakers, and pink-tinged lights lined the walls, casting the room in a serene, almost otherworldly glow. The scent of lilies and roses clogged the air, and suddenly the reality of what they were doing slammed into Stacy with the force of a freight train.

She stopped and clutched the back of one of the folding chairs to keep her shaking legs from buckling. It was hard to get enough oxygen, and her skin felt too tight for her body.

"Sis, are you okay?" Brenda asked, her expression concerned as she turned back to look at Stacy. She helped Stacy into a chair. "Just sit here for a minute and relax. You're white as a ghost. Let me see if they have some water."

Stacy wanted to thank her, wanted to get up and act like the adult she was expected to be today, but she only seemed to be able to stare at the coffin. The dark wood gleamed beneath the recessed lighting, her father's face just visible above the edge of the casket. He looked older than the last time she'd seen him, but peaceful on his white satin pillow, as if he were napping and not ... not ...

"Here." Brenda returned and crouched beside Stacy, pushing a plastic cup of water into her hands. "Believe me, I know how hard this is, but you need to hold it together, okay? Mom will be here any minute, and she needs us to be strong. Can I count on you, sis?"

She smoothed the hair back from Stacy's face. Somehow, Brenda had become the responsible sibling now, even though Stacy was older. Maybe it was a parent thing. Maybe it was the fact she was home and centered and had the support of a man who loved her. And maybe it was Brenda's kind soul, shining through the darkness.

Whatever it was, Stacy was grateful. She sipped

her water and nodded. "Yes, I'm good. Thank you, sis. I just needed a minute."

"I know." Tears shined in Brenda's eyes, and for a moment, the years disappeared and the sisters were back in their bedroom in the trailer, telling stories and gossiping about boys and planning their illustrious futures. "I love you, sis."

"I love you too." Stacy embraced Brenda tightly, hoping to convey all her emotions through the hug — love, gratefulness, loyalty. Once they separated, Stacy pulled a tissue from her pocket and dabbed her cheeks. "Now, let's get this funeral going before Mom starts fussing."

They both laughed and headed to the front of the room. Stacy set her purse aside then spent a moment paying her respects. The floral arrangement atop the casket was beautiful — red and white roses and a sleek golden banner proclaiming "Husband and Father."

Dad looked paler than usual but happy, a small smile on his face. Fresh tears welled in Stacy's eyes. Despite the pain and sorrow in her heart, she was happy her poor father was at rest at last. She'd harbored so much pain and anger because he'd lost his job and the changes that event wrought. Now it all seemed so pointless.

She leaned over and kissed his cheek, whispering, "I love you, Daddy. I'm sorry I wasn't here."

"Honey?"

Stacy turned to see her mother, looking much frailer than she remembered, pale and trembling in her black mourning suit. Overwhelming sadness engulfed her, and she rushed into her mother's arms, needing that comfort and closeness more than she needed her next breath. "Mom, I've missed you."

"I've missed you too, honey." Her mother sniffled then pulled back slightly to cup Stacy's cheeks. "Too bad it took something like this to get you to come home to us."

"I know. I'm sorry." She couldn't quite meet her mother's eyes. "I was hoping to spend more time with you before today. I know you've been busy with your friends. I didn't want to interfere with your routine or be a nuisance and —"

Her mother hugged her again, laughing. "Still a babbler when you're nervous, aren't you?" She squeezed Stacy tightly then let her go. "It's okay, honey. I have lots of friends, and they've been a great comfort. Sorry if I neglected you. The important thing is that you're here now and we're all together at last."

Stacy locked elbows with her mother, and they joined Brenda, Tommy and Sammy at the corner of the casket. The four adults stood side by side, arms around each other for support as mourners poured in for the service.

Three hours later, the receiving line finally cleared and everyone took their seats. Time stood still and sped up simultaneously. Stacy glanced toward the side of the room and spotted Reid standing near the wall. He looked so handsome in his suit and tie. She bit her tingling lips and imagined she could still taste him. He caught her eye and gave her a quick wink, letting her know he was thinking about her too.

Swallowing hard, Stacy focused on the pastor giving the eulogy at the lectern. Dad would've liked things today. He was always so gregarious and outgoing; he would've loved all these people gathering together to celebrate his life, even the tragic parts. She squeezed Brenda's arm then leaned in, resting her head on her mother's shoulder while she sobbed quietly into one of her father's old handkerchiefs. It must be comforting, Stacy thought, to have that small memento, that small reminder of their father's scent and presence, to keep with her now.

She sighed and closed her eyes, wishing for just one more day with her father, another chance to say a proper goodbye.

The minister finished a short prayer and then

slowly closed the lid on her father's casket. This was it, the last time she'd see Dad.

She'd done well up to this point in controlling her tears, but seeing that final gesture burst the dam wide open and she cried quietly into her tissue. Brenda did the same, Tommy's arm around her for comfort. What Stacy wouldn't have given at that moment to have Reid beside her, supporting her, loving her, caring for her. Then, as if by magic, he was there, sliding his arm around her shoulders, pulling her close to his chest as the gathered mourners stood to make their way out.

She buried her face in his warm chest and sobbed until there was nothing left inside her. All the while, he held her, stroking her hair and whispering soothing words against the top of her head. By the time Stacy raised her head, the room was empty except for her family and Reid.

"Okay?" he asked, tipping her chin up with his fingers. He gently cupped her cheeks and used his thumbs to wipe away her tears, his eyes so kind they nearly made her start crying all over again. Reid had always been so sweet to her. Even when he refused to tell her the truth.

Not trusting her voice, Stacy nodded and took a step back, straightening her clothes as best she could. This wasn't the time, but they hadn't talked about what had gone on with him and Gabby all those years ago, and Stacy felt it like a wedge between them. She still needed to be cautious. "We should get to the memorial lunch before people start to wonder."

"My staff has everything under control. Don't worry." Reid remained by her side as they walked out, hovering pleasantly near her without smothering her. She appreciated his warmth and strength, took comfort in the familiar scent of his musk cologne. Took comfort in everything about him, really.

The banquet hall was in another wing of the old mansion that was the funeral home and had been arranged as Stacy had prescribed at their meeting. The tables were immaculate. She couldn't have done any better herself.

"This looks great, Reid," she said, smiling. "Thank you. Dad would've loved it."

"My pleasure." He took her hand and squeezed it gently. "Anything I can do, just let me know."

Then he was off to supervise the staff at the buffet tables and greet the guests and basically make everyone feel comfortable, removing that burden from the grieving family. She and Brenda got their mother settled at a table, along with Sammy, then went to get food at the buffet tables.

Several people came up to offer their condolences.

Thank goodness Brenda was with her, because it had been so long and things were such a blur that Stacy couldn't have put a name to any of them.

"You doing okay, sis?" Brenda asked as they made their way down the buffet table. "You and Reid seem to be getting along better."

"Yeah, he's been great." She scooped out some of her father's favorite chicken Parmesan. "And so have you. In fact, everyone here in Boulder Point has been wonderful."

"Watch it, sis." Brenda chuckled. "Or I might start to think you missed us."

She *did* miss them. Here, at home, she felt she belonged, in a way she never had in Ohio. There, it was all about the work and climbing the corporate ladder. Here, at home, it was a true community, people who rallied around each other in times of trouble and grief. Except for Gabby, of course. She'd not made an appearance at the funeral, Stacy noticed. Good thing, because she wouldn't have been welcome.

They returned to their table, but Stacy was too excited to eat. They'd decided to have the luncheon before the private graveside service, but maybe that wasn't such a good idea. The finality of the burial loomed over her, squeezing out any thought of eating.

She gazed around the room, noticing most of the

folks had also helped them after her father had lost his job too. She hadn't remembered until today that they'd cooked and cleaned and even taken up a collection to make sure the bills were paid each month, and the kids had clothes and food. Columbus was a nice city, but there wasn't anyone there she could depend on. Not like that.

People finished their meals, and the funeral director entered the room and nodded. Brenda leaned over to Stacy and whispered, "They're ready to take Dad to the cemetery."

CHAPTER 12

Ginny had left the funeral home before the luncheon, wanting to get back to the inn. Funerals were still hard for her, and as she walked the few blocks back to her home, she couldn't help feeling melancholy.

She'd not missed the way Stacy and Reid looked at each other when they thought no one saw. She and Donald used to gaze at one another that way. Full of love and hope, and promise and devotion. Seeing it again was bittersweet. Brought back how much she'd had in her life and how much she'd lost.

Waiting at the corner for the light to change, she couldn't help thinking what a shame it was that Stacy would leave Saturday to return to Ohio. Just when she and Reid seemed on course to get back together. Plus, having Stacy around made Ginny's life a tad less lonesome, and her help with the wedding had been invaluable. Perhaps there was a way she could persuade her to stick around Boulder Point and take the event-planner position.

On the way home, Ginny stopped in at her favorite antique shop on Main Street. Needful Things had become her go-to spot for décor, and she'd become something of a regular. Today she was on the lookout for an antique wedding cake topper for Maisie to use on the cake for the upcoming wedding reception. Stacy had suggested it during their meeting in the library, and Ginny had immediately loved the idea.

"Lovely to see you." Vera Newport, the shop owner, greeted Ginny from behind the front counter. "Did you come from John Brighton's funeral?"

"I did." Ginny smiled. "It was a lovely service."

"I'm so sorry I had to miss it," Vera said. "But I had no one else to look after the place, and I hate to lock the doors during tourist season."

"The floral arrangement you sent was beautiful. Mrs. Brighton asked me to thank you when I saw you." Ginny glanced around at all the out-of-towners milling about the place. There were a few locals, too, including Charlie Hanson, an old sea captain who looked as if he'd stepped right off a bag of Gorton's fish sticks. In addition to his commercial fishing business, he also ran a charter fishing service and drove tourists to and from the airport to make ends meet.

"Ladies," Charlie said, stepping up to the counter. "How's the first guest going, Ginny?"

"Good. Stacy's been very sweet. She even helped me with some wedding planning for this summer."

"That's sweet," Vera said.

"Yep." Charlie grinned, hiking his chin upward. "Seen Dooley yet?"

"Dooley?" Ginny frowned.

"The ghost inhabiting that inn of yours. He's haunted the place for years. Been known to pull a few shenanigans now and then to scare folks off." Charlie winked. "Then again, if he's put up with you renovating his home, chances are he likes you and wants you to stay."

Ginny scoffed at the idea. "Don't be silly. There's no such thing as ghosts. Even if there were, I wouldn't tell anybody if I saw one. They'd think I was crazy. And I've put far too much into this new life and new business to let some spook frighten me away."

Still, as she left the shop and passed a display of antique salt and pepper shakers, Ginny couldn't help wondering if perhaps this Dooley hadn't paid her a visit after all.

CHAPTER 13

Reid stuck around the funeral home to clean up after the luncheon. The graveside service was private, and Stacy had her family for support, so he'd made himself scarce when the time came. He didn't want to come across as overbearing. Whatever was happening between them was too new, too raw, too tender. Even though he had only a few days to win Stacy over, he didn't want to risk destroying things before they'd even had a chance to start by insinuating himself where he wasn't wanted.

As he collected garbage and swept the floor of the banquet room, he couldn't help wondering what life might have been like if he'd given it all up and gone to Ohio with her all those years ago.

Not that he didn't love his life in Boulder Point. It was just that Stacy's return had gotten him thinking.

Maybe if he'd left, he'd have found a way to put himself through school or joined the culinary institute. Maybe gotten his degree and opened a fancy eatery in the heart of Columbus. Maybe he'd have garnered nationwide praise for his dishes and catered to the same celebrity clientele that Stacy's firm enjoyed.

But there was the other problem. Gabby. Maybe if he'd told her the truth, she'd have understood why he felt he had to protect Gabby, why he defended her even when he opposed her actions and behavior toward Stacy.

He sighed and handed off his full garbage bag to one of his staff then started a fresh one.

Then again, they'd both been so young, so inexperienced in life, things could very well have been a royal disaster. Well, more of a disaster than they'd ended up being between them at the end. Their breakup had been difficult and painful, making him wary of falling in love again. The truth was he couldn't fall in love again with someone else. The whole time, he'd still been in love with Stacy.

Reid felt he'd made progress in getting Stacy to at least consider the possibility of a life back in her hometown. Plus, he'd seen that look on her face when her family had been together. That wasn't the face of a woman eager to flee.

"Hey, son. How're things going here?" his father asked, walking into the banquet room. "Looks like you guys have cleanup under control."

"Yep." Reid straightened and looked around as his staff bustled to get everything put away and tidied up. He really did have the best group of people working for him. He was grateful for them every single day. "We aim to please."

"Does that include Stacy Brighton? You trying to please her too?"

Reid gave his father a puzzled look. "What are you talking about? Her family hired us to cater this event, and that's what we did."

"C'mon, son." His dad clapped him on the shoulder. "That's not what I'm talking about, and you know it. I saw the way you two looked at each other during her father's funeral. Just promise me you'll be careful, okay? You know what happened between me and your mom."

Reid frowned. "Seriously, Dad. There's nothing going on between us."

Liar.

He wasn't ready to share that with anyone yet. Even his father.

"Look, son. I like Stacy, always have. But I'd hate to see you make the same mistakes I did. Don't spend your life pining for the one that got away. That's all I'm saying." He sighed. "You're a single, successful businessman. There're plenty of women who'd love to be with a guy like you. Think about it, son. Your mom wasn't the only one who made mistakes in our relationship. I made my share too. Sometimes you just have to give up the blame game and move on."

He walked away, leaving Reid to stand alone, staring after him.

"Hey," Gabby said, stepping in beside him. "You all right?"

He nodded, still lost in thought over his father's words.

"Listen, I didn't mean to eavesdrop, but I couldn't help hearing what your dad had to say, and I've got a different perspective."

Reid exhaled and gave Gabby a sideways glance. The last thing he needed was advice from the woman who'd gotten him into this whole mess in the first place. "I can't wait."

She crossed her arms and frowned. "Look, I know one of the reasons that you and Stacy broke up was because of me. And I know I treated her really bad in high school after everything that happened with my dad and your mom and ... well. I just don't want you to lose another chance at happiness because of me."

"What are you saying, Gabs?" Reid asked, straightening.

"I'm saying that I owe you one for the other night at the bar." Gabby shrugged one shoulder as she tucked a hank of dark hair behind her ear. "I'm not saying that you tell her everything about, you know ... us. Me. But I'm saying that I'm sorry for how I treated her. She didn't deserve it. Bruce and I are trying to work things out, and so far, so good. We're happy again. And I'd love for you to find that same happiness with someone, Reid. If Stacy's truly the woman you love and want to be with for the rest of your life, you should go for it."

He exhaled slowly and narrowed his gaze. "Fine. But I think you need to tell Stacy about being sorry for bullying her in school."

Gabby sighed and stared down at the linoleum for a few seconds and then nodded. "Maybe I will."

STACY and her family had wanted to stay together for a few more hours after the emotional graveside service, so they had the limo drop them at her mother's trailer. Tommy's car was there because he'd driven their mother to the funeral home. He'd give Stacy a ride back to pick her car up later.

They pulled up outside the trailer, and Stacy got out first to help her mother, while Tommy took care of Brenda and Sammy on the other side. Fresh tears stung her eyes before Stacy blinked them away. She'd thought she'd finished crying by now, but there were still more tears to come.

The day was warm and sunny, so instead of going inside right away, they gathered at the picnic table under the large oak tree in the front yard. Bees buzzed, and chickadees chirped. The smell of freshly mown grass spiced the humid summer air. House wrens and goldfinches fluttered past on their way to the feeder, much to Sammy's squealed delight.

After the chaos and heartache of the morning, things felt peaceful here.

Stacy took a deep breath and rolled her stiff neck, enjoying the prickle of sunshine on her skin, finally chasing away the cold that had seeped into her bones at the cemetery.

"Stacy, honey," her mother said, her voice as quiet as the passing breeze. "I know you always wondered why your dad and I never moved out of this place. I think it's time I explained."

"No, Mom." Stacy reached over and took her

hand. "You don't have to explain anything to me. Especially not right now."

"I want to." Her mother took a deep breath. "Once your dad got laid off, our values changed. We didn't need the money anymore. What we really wanted was to spend time with you girls and experience and enjoy life." She gave a sad little smile. "When your father had that corporate job, he was always so stressed and angry, only home to change clothes and sleep. He missed out on a lot of you girls growing up because he was at work all the time. After he lost the job, he was happier. In fact, I think it was the best thing that ever happened to him."

"It's true," Brenda said, taking a seat beside Stacy and putting her hand over Stacy's. "Sometimes money and prestige aren't everything."

Stacy stared down at their hands clasped atop the table, remembering those years from her childhood. At the time, she'd been so wrapped up in her own life and problems she hadn't paid much attention to how her father's unemployment had affected everyone else in the family.

Now, though, looking back, she could see her mother was right. Dad had smiled more after he'd stopped working for corporate. He'd had more time to help with their homework or spend time lazing around the house with their mother. They'd seemed truly happy and in love.

"Wait here a minute," her mother said, heading toward the trailer. "I've got something to give you girls." She returned a few moments later with something in her hand. "It's time I passed these along."

In her palm were two rings — not fancy, just wide sterling silver bands etched with designs. She gave one to Brenda and one to Stacy. Brenda's featured a wave design embellished on it, while Stacy's had tiny fireflies etched into its surface.

"Your father gave those to me on our fifteenth and twenty-fifth wedding anniversaries. Even though your dad couldn't buy me expensive jewelry, he was so good to me in all the ways that count. Those rings symbolize all the things we loved together — the fireflies from that field beside the inn, the ocean, this town. I want you girls to have them now, because I wish all those things for you. Brenda, you and Tommy are so happy together. I want the same for you, Stacy. I wish you both could have the same wonderful life I had with your father."

Stacy clutched the firefly ring tight in her hand, unable to put it on her finger just yet.

She hugged her mother, seeing things in a new light. The trailer park wasn't a prison, but a peaceful paradise. Their home hadn't been big or fancy, but her mother always kept it neat and comfortable. And their lot sat near the forest, with a brook nearby. Small but decorated like an oasis, with lush greenery, vibrant flowers, and plenty of trees.

Truly lovely.

Her thoughts drifted to Reid and how attentive he'd been at the funeral, how caring and loyal and protective. Not for the first time since setting foot back in Boulder Point, Stacy couldn't help wondering if perhaps she'd had her priorities wrong from the start. Perhaps they could reconcile. And maybe all those years ago Reid had been right, that Boulder Point was a fine place to live a lifetime.

Perhaps she could ask for more time away from her job to get to know him and the town better. But could she live with knowing he'd once chosen another woman and this town over her?

CHAPTER 14

By the time Stacy made it back to the funeral home later that day, everything from the memorial luncheon had been packed and removed. The only thing left was Reid and his truck. He waited by his vehicle as Tommy dropped her off, then waved her over. "How are you holding up, Sunshine?"

"Okay." She walked up to him, and he battled the urge to take her into his arms and just hold her for a while. She looked asleep on her feet, her normally creamy skin pale, and dark circles shadowing her eyes.

Seemed the emotional burden of the day had finally taken its toll. In fact, Stacy looked nearly as exhausted as he felt.

She gave him a strained smile and held her hand over her eyes to shield them from the late-afternoon sun. "We went back to Mom's trailer after the grave-side service. It was nice, being back home again."

"Good. I'm glad to hear you finally reconnected. She's missed you." His blue gaze narrowed, and he exhaled slowly, his fatigue making him feel more vulnerable than he liked. "We all have."

"Yeah?" She raised an inquiring brow at him. "Who's we?"

He did his best to tamp down the burst of joy her teasing conjured, and failed miserably.

"Oh, you know. Floyd down at the hardware store. Principal Griffin from the high school," he teased back. She smacked him on the arm, and he slid his arm around her shoulders and pulled her tighter to his side. It was so good to see her happy again, despite the solemnity of the day. "What are your plans for this evening?"

"Not much." Stacy shrugged. "Figured I'd go back to the inn, change clothes, relax."

"How about spending it with me?" Reid asked, surprising himself. He'd planned to return to The Tuckaway and help with dinner service, but Bruce was there and could handle things on his own tonight. Wasn't that what assistants were for?

Reid would text him later to be sure. "Come on, it'll be fun. We can revisit some of our old haunts. I can show you the new things in town. It'll be fun — and relaxing — I promise."

Tired as she was — she sagged against him — she agreed. "Okay."

"Awesome." His energy level suddenly soared. "I'll follow you back to the inn so you can drop off your car and change. Then we can take my truck."

"Perfect."

Half an hour later, as he sat outside the Firefly Inn, waiting for Stacy, he texted Bruce, who not only willingly offered to handle everything that night, but wished him well with Stacy. He was a good man, and Reid was glad he and Gabby were working things out.

About time someone took the duty of guarding Gabs off his hands.

He set his phone aside as Stacy climbed back into the truck.

"Where are we off to first?" she asked, looking adorable in her pink T-shirt and jeans. She'd scrubbed off her makeup and pulled her hair back into a low ponytail. She looked as if she'd finally gotten her second wind.

"I should change too, if that's okay." He started the engine and pulled out of the circle drive. "My house isn't far from here."

"Great." She slid her sunglasses on then stared out

the window beside her as they headed down the town's main drag. Every so often, Reid hazarded a glance at her. That was when he spotted the necklace.

"Isn't that your mom's old ring?" he asked.

She clasped the sliver band gently. "Yeah. She gave it to me today at the trailer. Brenda got one too. She said Dad got them for her for their wedding anniversaries to remind them of the things they loved. Mine has fireflies on it because she knows I always thought they were magical. Brenda's is waves because she's like a mermaid when it comes to the ocean."

"Wow." Reid smiled, touched by the story. "Your parents were always crazy about each other."

"Yeah." Her voice took on that wistful tone again, the one that tugged at his heart. "Funny, but I never paid that much attention until now."

Unable to resist any longer, he reached over and took her hand. "Death has a way of making people see the things they normally miss."

"True." She sniffled and then laughed. "Just look at me, back here again."

He squeezed her hand and turned off onto the quiet street downtown where his bungalow sat. His home wasn't some big, fancy showpiece, but it was clean and well cared for, and he loved it. Someday he hoped to start a family here. Reid laced his fingers with

Stacy's as they pulled beside the curb in front of his home.

"Is this where you live?"

"It is." He cut the engine and stared at the dark-green-and-white Cape Cod exterior with the two rockers on the porch. "Want to come in for a minute?"

She looked at him, and for a second he thought she'd say yes, but then those old barriers dropped back into place, and he knew she wouldn't. "Oh, you won't be long, right? I'll stay here."

Disappointment pinched his chest, but Reid was a patient man. He'd wait until she was ready, however long that might be. His father's words about pining after the one who got away chased through his mind before he pushed them aside. That wasn't him, and this was different. Now, if he could just get Gabby and Stacy to talk, he'd be all set. "Sure. No problem. Be right out then."

He all but ran inside, stripped and changed in record time, and was ready again in less than ten minutes. He might be patient, but he wasn't stupid. No way was he leaving Stacy alone any longer than necessary. He didn't want her changing her mind about spending more time with him.

Reid made sure he had his wallet, phone, and keys then returned to the truck. This time, he walked up to

Stacy's open window and said, "Beach is only about a block or so over. Walking might do us both some good. Stretch our legs after all that standing around earlier."

Stacy nodded and got out, keeping the sunglasses on so her eyes were hidden from him. Still, the longer they walked, the more her melancholy lifted, and every so often, she'd touch the firefly ring on the chain around her neck. Was she thinking about her parents' happy relationship? Was she thinking, like him, about what they'd once shared too? Reid glanced over at her and smiled. "Care to share?"

She shrugged and looked out over the ocean in the distance. "Nothing. Just remembering all the fun times we had in town."

He led her across the street to where sand met pavement. They each kicked off their shoes and dug their toes into the warm sand. "Remember when we snuck up on Tina Mae and her new boyfriend over that dune while they were ... *otherwise occupied*?"

Stacy laughed. "Oh my gosh, yes! Talk about surprised. I've never seen two people streak down a beach faster in my life."

"Me neither." He pointed to a line of trees down the way. "And over there's that pine where we carved our initials in eighth grade."

"I bet there isn't a spot in town we haven't marked in one way or another."

"True." He started toward the shoreline with Stacy at his side. "But some things have changed around here."

The water sparkled, and the gulls screeched, the smell of brine filling the air. He took her elbow to steer her around a patch of seaweed, and she gave him a fond grin, which he felt all the way to his toes.

"I'd forgotten what a gentleman you are, Reid Callahan." Stacy lifted her sunglasses to give him a wink. "Even if you do drive like a bat out of hell sometimes."

"Me?" he said with mock affront. "Trust me. You do not want to go there, missy. I remember your first driving test and a certain instructor who refused to ride with you ever again."

"Eh." She scoffed. "He was a pansy."

"He was the high school football coach."

"Then he should've been used to a rough ride."

They both cracked up, making their way along the shore, dodging waves as they went.

It all felt so right, so perfect, that Reid never wanted it to end.

They approached the rocks again, and Reid

stopped, turning to face her. "Have I told you how much I admire you, Sunshine?"

"Huh?" She scrunched her face, confused. "Why?"

"Because of your strength and your intelligence and your genuinely good heart. You've always been so brave, holding it all together." He took her hands, frowning. "If I lost my dad, I'm not sure what I'd do."

She hung her head. "You're wrong. I'm not strong or smart. And right now I'm questioning my good heart."

Now it was his turn to look flummoxed. "You can't be serious."

"I am." She perched on a nearby boulder. "I can't help feeling guilty. I wasn't here for Dad. I missed so much time with him, missed so many chances to make amends."

Reid cupped her cheek, forcing her to meet his gaze, stroking his thumb over her soft skin. "But you're here now. That's the important thing."

"Is it?" She slid her sunglasses to the top of her head and sighed. "I just don't know anymore."

"It is." Giving in to his riptide of emotion at last, he leaned in and kissed her softly before pulling back slightly. "You hungry?"

It seemed to take her a moment to process his question, but her stomach apparently picked up on it right away, because it grumbled loudly. Reid chuckled. He was starving, and he'd not seen her eat much at the luncheon, so he guessed she must be famished too.

"I am," she said, smiling. "Do you want to go back into town and grab something?"

"Nah." He took her hand and led her back the way they'd come. "I figured we could grab dinner at The Clam Dunk then sit on the seawall while we ate. Like old times, right?"

Her eyes widened in delight. "Perfect! I haven't had a decent clam roll in years."

They placed their order at the small seafood shack window and then waited for their food. Tourists milled about the beach, and amateur fishermen lined both sides of the seawall. They found an empty spot and took a seat on the warm cement, their bare feet dangling over the edge as the sun began to set. They breathed in the smell of fried food and listened to the crash of waves.

Stacy moaned in ecstasy after her first bite and got him to thinking about all sorts of things besides food. Then he took a bite of his own clam roll — all peppery breaded clams and tangy pickle-packed tartar sauce on a toasted burger bun — and he did some hungry-man groaning of his own. It was no wonder The Clam Dunk was legendary in these parts.

"This is so good!" Stacy said, wiping her mouth with a napkin. "Haven't had one of these since I left Boulder Point."

"I know, right?" He swallowed another bite, washing it down with his soda. "I've been trying to steal their recipe for years."

"How dastardly of you," Stacy said with mock horror.

"Hey, a businessman's gotta do what a businessman's gotta do." He finished off his sandwich and then leaned back on his hands. "You should really consider Ginny's offer to work at the inn. We could use someone with your talents around here."

Stacy put her trash back into her bag as she gave a one-shoulder shrug. "That would be nice, but it's a lot less money than I'm making now."

"And a lot less stress and responsibility," Reid pointed out.

"True." The hint of thoughtfulness in her tone gave him hope. Maybe she was thinking along the same lines. She stood and tossed their trash in a nearby bin.

"Well, I should get back to the inn," Stacy said. "I'm so tired I can hardly see straight, and I need to be up early in the morning to help Brenda and Mom go through all of Dad's paperwork and affairs."

"Right." He pushed to his feet as well and took her hand again. "I'll take you back now, under one condition."

She peered up at him, so cute Reid couldn't resist stealing one more kiss. Afterward, Stacy stepped back and smiled.

"What condition?" she asked.

"Have dinner with me again tomorrow night."

STACY HAD NEVER BEEN SO EXHAUSTED. After Reid dropped her at the inn, she managed to slog her way through a quick shower then put on her pajamas and flop into bed. Her swirling emotions, however, kept her from sleeping despite her fatigue. Sadness over her father weighed her down like an anchor, and she missed the easy camaraderie with her family earlier. Most of all, though, she missed Reid.

And that terrified her.

She'd come so close to believing in him once, fallen hard for him, only to find out too late that she wasn't as important to him as she'd thought. He'd let her go, and if what she'd heard was true, it hadn't taken him long to replace her. With Gabby. What was to say he wouldn't do it again when it came time for her to leave Saturday?

Their time together at the beach had been beyond amazing — so sweet and fun and lighthearted. Exactly what she'd needed to take her mind off the gloom of the funeral and all the work still to be done.

She clasped the firefly ring again, laying her hand over her heart. Since she'd been home, the aching hollowness in her chest had slowly dissolved, replaced now by warmth from being close to her mother and her sister again.

Mom had been right earlier. They'd all been happier after Dad had left that corporate nightmare behind and worked closer to home. She'd just been too blind to see it back then. Yes, they'd lost some prestige in the community, but they'd gained so much more in other ways. And so what if shallow people like Gabby didn't understand her family or their situation? That was her loss, not Stacy's.

As she stared up at the ceiling, a muffled curse echoed through the door. It sounded as if it was coming from the library downstairs. No one had been around when Stacy returned to the inn, so she'd assumed Ginny had gone to bed.

Curious, she got up and padded quietly toward the

door. Maybe Ginny was still up and needed help with her wedding. Silently, she crept downstairs and peered around the corner into the library.

Sure enough, Ginny sat at the long table, even more papers piled around her than before. Poor thing. Stacy had seen her earlier at her father's funeral but never got the chance to thank her for coming. She knocked softly on the doorframe so as not to startle Ginny.

"Hey, you're working late tonight," Stacy said.

"Oh, hello." Ginny looked up and gave her a tired smile. "Yes. I got to thinking today that we'll need a contingency plan for seating in case it rains. I'm having the devil of a time trying to figure out where to put everyone, though."

"Here." Stacy walked in and stood beside Ginny's chair to see the plans. "Let's see. If you can get your hands on some rental tents, you can set them up over the fabulous outdoor patio that overlooks the ocean. That will help with part of the crowd. It's perfect because the fireflies in the field will add their own magical light show." Stacy curled her fist around the ring on the chain. Childhood memories of chasing fireflies and later memories of kissing Reid in that same field, the fireflies blinking around them, brought a smile to her lips. She looked down at the plans again.

"What about the conservatory? Three sets of French doors lead outside, which will give us plenty of traffic control. And, if worse comes to worst, we can set up tables in the conservatory, put the tent up over the patio, and create our own little oasis. We can even do a covered walkway so guests never have to get wet."

"Sounds brilliant," Ginny said, nose wrinkling. "Except I haven't had a chance to renovate the conservatory yet. I'm not sure there's enough time to get everything ready."

"Let's go see." Stacy followed Ginny to the opposite side of the inn. The place still looked in pretty fine condition, given its age. You could still see the delicate stencil work on the white walls, and the black-and-white marble floor still gleamed beneath their feet. Sure, there were a few areas of peeling paint, but nothing a bit of elbow grease wouldn't fix. "I think this is totally doable. I'll even help you get started before I leave, if you like. When I'm not helping my mom and sister, that is."

"Oh, I'd love that!" Ginny pulled Stacy in for a quick hug just as something darted across the patio and into the gardens. A cat, maybe?

Stacy leaned back and cocked her head toward the French doors. "I think your uninvited guest is back."

Ginny blanched for a second before giving a nervous giggle. "I'm sorry?"

"The rabbit in your garden. Or it might be a cat. What did you think I was talking about?"

"Oh, nothing. I hope I don't have a pest problem. And I wouldn't know what to do with a stray cat." Ginny wandered to the doors and peered out. "Well, you better get some sleep. It's getting late, and I'm sure you have another busy day ahead tomorrow."

"Are you sure? If you have more plans to go over, I'm happy to help."

"Nonsense, dear." Ginny put her arm around Stacy's shoulders and guided her toward the door. "I can figure out the rest of it on my own. And I've decided to put an ad in the local paper for my event-planner position. Hopefully someone will respond soon and I won't have to bother you for any more help."

Stacy couldn't help feeling a stab of regret at the thought of another person getting the job Ginny had offered her, but there was no way she could make ends meet with the salary offered for the position. It was less than half of what she was currently making. And yes, her living expenses would be less in Boulder Point, but there were other issues like insurance and taxes and credit card bills. The lifestyle she maintained in Columbus didn't come cheap.

As she climbed back upstairs to her room, Stacy listened to the crash of the ocean waves and relished the cool breeze drifting in through the open windows. It would be so lovely to live and work here amongst this gorgeous scenery and these kind people and her family and Reid.

She grabbed her laptop and climbed onto her bed to check her email. Her inbox was jammed with a slew of work messages. She moved them all into a separate folder to read later. This was her bereavement time, a special leave to process her grief and get back in touch with her family. She refused to let her job interfere with that now, no matter how persistent.

Frowning, she scrolled through the rest of her messages, feeling the weight of her mother's firefly ring press heavier on her chest as if an unseen hand had touched it. She clasped the precious memento, needing to feel that connection with her family again, especially tonight.

IN THE LIBRARY, Ginny took her seat once more. She'd exaggerated a bit about needing assistance with the wedding, but she'd needed to give Stacy a reason to stay in Boulder Point. Her family was here, but sometimes that wasn't enough for people. Ginny, on the other hand, knew how hard things could be on your own. There were times she'd give just about anything to have her family back again.

She sighed and gathered her paperwork together. Too bad Stacy hadn't made a firm decision to stay. Ginny would've loved to hire her as her event planner, and from what she'd seen at the funeral today, Reid Callahan was well and truly smitten again. It would be nice for those two to have another chance.

Meddling wasn't her style, though. She preferred to simply give things a gentle push in the right direction.

Once she'd straightened the table and put her things away, she shut the lights and then wandered the house one last time to secure it for the night. She walked into the conservatory then out onto the patio. The night was cool, and the salty air wafted around her, the breeze refreshing. Barn swallows swooped through the air, scooping up the insects that came out at dusk. A faint cry issued from the shadows.

Ginny glanced over to see two golden eyes gleaming at her through the darkness. The stray Stacy had seen? She walked toward them, but the eyes disappeared.

She really hoped it wasn't a cat, because Ginny hadn't been kidding. She had no idea how to care for one. Plus, if she started feeding the cat now, it would come to depend on her, and she couldn't handle that right now, not after losing Donald. Shaking her head, she walked back inside and secured the French doors in the conservatory. Hopefully, if it was a stray, it would find its way home.

On her way to bed, she peeked into the dining room to make sure everything was set for breakfast in the morning. When she switched on the light, all the salt and pepper shakers she'd put on the tables earlier were gone. Perplexed, she stepped closer to the nearest table. No one else had been around tonight except for her and Stacy, and she hadn't removed them.

A creak issued near the far wall, and Ginny glanced over to find all the shakers lined neatly on the sideboard. Her heart skipped a beat.

How the ...

Charlie Hanson's conversation from the antique store rang through her head.

Seen Dooley yet?

Even a few hours ago, the notion of spirits from another realm seemed silly. Now, she wasn't quite so sure. Still, she steeled her courage and put the salt and pepper shakers back where they belonged before shutting the light and heading into the hall. For good measure, she looked back over her shoulder as she exited. "Take that, Dooley! I won't let you ruin things for me."

Just as she switched off the light, one of the windows near the front of the dining room slammed open, banging hard against the wall. The curtain blew in the whistling wind, sounding distinctly like a man's deep laugh.

Ginny froze for a moment before brushing off her ridiculous imagination. *Ghosts aren't real.* Maisie must've had the window open earlier when she was baking and forgot to latch it. Yep. That explained it. Still, she turned on the lights once more to close the window before rushing to bed in record time.

CHAPTER 15

"Order whatever you like, Mom," Stacy said, perusing the lunch menu at The Tuckaway Grill. They'd worked hard all morning and had gotten a surprising amount done.

Stacy's organizational skills had been put to good use, assigning each of them a certain area to work in — Brenda had gone through all the old files and paperwork in Dad's office; Mom had packed up his clothes and other belongings; and Stacy had handled all the necessary phone calls to the credit card companies, Social Security, and insurance companies.

Luckily, the county coroner's office had come through with the copies of the death certificate in a timely manner, so there'd been no delay in getting them faxed in either.

Tommy had had to work again, so Brenda had

brought Sammy along. He'd turned out to be a welcome distraction from their tiresome, gloomy tasks. She smiled over at her sister now and waggled her fingers at her squirming nephew, who sat firmly trapped on Brenda's lap while the hostess went to get a high chair. "And you too, Bren. Get my Sammy whatever he wants."

"What he wants right now is a spank on the rear if he doesn't sit still." Brenda's kiss on her son's cheek removed any real threat or sting from her words. "You don't have to buy our lunch, Stace."

"I know. But I want to. It's the least I can do after how wonderful you all have been to me." Once more, that pang of regret filled Stacy's chest. She really needed to come home more often from now on. Time passed too quickly. "Believe it or not, I'm going to miss this place."

"Well," her mother said, taking each of her daughters' hands. "I'm so thrilled to have my family back together at last. Even under the circumstances, it's been so wonderful having both of you girls with me. I don't know what I would've done without you. Your dad must be looking down from heaven and smiling on us."

"He would've loved this," Brenda said, sniffling.

"Yeah." Stacy's eyes stung with unshed tears.

"I wish you could stay longer," her mother continued, getting teary-eyed herself. "It's too bad you have to leave so soon."

A stab of longing pierced Stacy's chest. She wished she could stay longer too. For her family. For her peace of mind.

"Don't weeve, Auntie Stace!" Sammy cried, wriggling out of his mother's embrace and rushing to Stacy with his arms raised. She picked him up, and he clung to her neck. "You home with us!"

His toddler expression was so stern that all three women laughed.

Brenda took her son back, shaking her head. "Sammy, honey, we talked about this. Auntie Stace has to go back to Ohio, where she lives. What about her work?"

"Ladies," Reid said, stopping by their table. "How's everything today?"

"Good," Stacy said, not meeting his gaze. All she could think about when she looked at him was their kiss, and she couldn't afford to think about that right now. "Thanks for asking."

"My pleasure," he said, his hand coming to rest on her shoulder. And was it her imagination, or had his voice lowered over those words, gone a bit rough and sexy, as if he'd meant that only for her? She shook off the ridiculous thought. A few kisses and snuggles did not a relationship make. Her mother and Brenda exchanged a look Stacy didn't miss.

"Can I get anyone a refill on their drinks?" Reid asked, massaging Stacy's stiff muscles. "Your food should be ready shortly."

"I'd love another soda," her mother said. "And don't you look dapper today, Reid Callahan? Doesn't he, Stacy?"

Unable to avoid eye contact any longer, she swiftly glanced sideways at him. Faded jeans, a brown blazer, and a crisp white button-down shirt. Yep. Dapper was one way to describe the guy. Drool-worthy gorgeous was another. It should be illegal for a man to look so good and still be so kind. She nodded. "Yes, he looks nice."

"Such high praise," Reid said, his tone dripping with amusement. "Not sure I can handle all these extravagant compliments."

His sarcasm helped eased her tension, and Stacy relaxed a bit. "And here I thought you fished for lobster, not compliments."

Brenda snorted, and Reid chuckled. Their mother gave Stacy a stop-it-that's-not-nice stare.

"I'll get your soda, Mrs. Brighton," Reid said, taking her glass and walking away.

It took all Stacy's willpower not to watch him go, not to admire the way the soft wool clung to his broad shoulders or the snug fit of those faded jeans against his taut, firm —

"So, how are things going there, sis?" Brenda asked, her brow raised.

"What?" Stacy frowned. It took her a minute to haul her thoughts back to their conversation. "Oh. You mean with Reid? Fine, I guess."

"Only fine?" Her sister grinned. "Looked like a whole lot more than fine to me. I practically got scorched from all the electricity sparking between you two just now."

"Reid always was such a nice boy. I never understood why things didn't work out between you two," her mother said.

"It's complicated." Stacy sat back as Reid returned with her mother's refill.

"What's complicated?" he asked, giving Stacy a wink.

"Nothing," she said, heat flaring in her cheeks.

His expression told her he didn't quite believe her, but he let it drop anyway, thankfully. "What time should I pick you up tonight, Sunshine?" he asked.

"Are you two going on a date?" her mother and Brenda asked in unison, their eyes alight with interest.

"Yes," Reid said.

"No," Stacy said. "He's just taking me out to eat."

"Sounds like a date to me," her mother said.

"Me too." Brenda smiled.

"Are you gonna marry Auntie Stace?" Sammy asked, scowling at Reid.

To his credit, Reid had the decency to look stunned. "Oh, well, I —"

"No, honey. He's just taking me to dinner. That's it." Stacy clutched the firefly ring around her neck like a lifeline. She stared at the tabletop, refusing to meet Reid's gaze, even though his glance weighed heavy on her.

Finally he cleared his throat and stepped back. "I'll, uh, go check on your order then, ladies. Enjoy the rest of your visit to The Tuckaway."

Brenda kicked her hard under the table. "Why weren't you nice to him, sis?"

"Ow!" She rubbed her sore shin and glared at her sister. "I was nice to him. And thanks for putting us on the spot."

"What?" Brenda shrugged, sliding Sammy around into the high chair the hostess brought to keep him from fussing. "I only asked if you two were dating. You've gone out with him a couple of times since you've been back in town. You're both single and obviously still attracted to each other. I don't see what the problem is."

"The problem is that I live halfway across the country from him. And there's unfinished business between us."

"Unfinished, huh?" She sipped her soda. "Well, you best get that taken care of before you leave. Of course, one of you could always move. Or you could do things long-distance for a while."

"I'm not sure the issues between us are the sort of thing you just quickly get over," Stacy said, crossing her arms and feeling entirely too vulnerable. Was she being unreasonable? That had been *ten years* ago. Reid had been just a boy. He was grown up now; they both were.

It was stupid to hold onto her anger about Gabby, but Stacy couldn't help feeling there was still something there. Something that needed to be resolved before they could move forward. And what exactly did *move forward* mean, anyway? "Besides, we each have our own lives now. Neither of us can just up and leave. It would never work."

"It might work," Brenda said, opening a package of saltines for Sammy to munch on while they waited for their food.

"I don't know ..."

Reid returned with their meals. He gave Stacy that little half smile of his that made her toes curl inside her sneakers, and began setting out their plates — burgers and fries all around, except for Sammy, who had toasted cheese. "Everything look okay, ladies?"

"Yes, Reid. Thank you," her mother gushed. "We were just telling Stacy what a nice boy you always were and how we've missed seeing you two together."

"Aw, that's very sweet of you, Mrs. Brighton," he said, his gaze never leaving Stacy. "I'll leave you to your lunch then. And Stacy, I'll pick you up tonight at seven thirty. Will that work?"

She nodded, not trusting her voice.

After he left the table, she exhaled slowly and squirted ketchup and mustard on her burger. Bad enough she lit up like a light bulb whenever the guy was around. Now she had to go and do it in front of her family. They'd be all over her about rekindling her relationship with Reid, and there wasn't anything she could do about it.

"So," Brenda said after tearing her son's cheese toast into bite-sized pieces for him and devouring a couple of her fries. "What are your plans for tomorrow, sis? You've only a few more days in Boulder Point. Or do you need to check with Reid first?"

"Ha ha. Very funny." Stacy took a big bite of

burger, grateful for something to fill her mouth so she didn't have to answer right away. After she swallowed, she wiped her mouth. The food was delicious, of course. The burger was cooked to perfection, and the toppings fresh and crisp. Add in the salt-and-vinegar-flavored fries, and it was a small bite of heaven. The thought of leaving Boulder Point was becoming less appealing. "I have no plans for tomorrow, as a matter of fact, other than finishing up what we didn't get done today of Dad's stuff."

"How about if we have a nice girls-only celebration," Brenda said. "A new spa just opened on Main Street, and I've heard really great things about it from my friends. I can book us all a spa day tomorrow — manicures, pedicures, facials, massages, the works."

"Oh, that sounds divine!" Stacy said around another bite of burger. "I'm in dire need of a pedi, and my neck's been sore since I left Columbus." She didn't tell them about her accident with Reid messing up her alignment — in more ways than one. "Let's do it. Mom, are you okay with going?"

"Absolutely. I was looking at some funky new blue nail polish when I was out the other day, and I think it might be just the thing for my summer toes."

Stacy's heart warmed at the way her mother was putting on an everything-is-fine act. She knew deep down her mother was devastated at her father's death. But acting as though things were okay was half the battle. Her mother would be fine in the long run, and that gave Stacy comfort.

"Perfect!" Brenda grinned. "I'll call when I get home and make the reservations. And Stacy, you can let Reid know tonight on your date that you're spending tomorrow with us."

Stacy snorted and tossed a fry at her sister, which Sammy caught midair and shoved in his mouth. Yep. The kid was definitely a Brighton. Quick on his feet and fast on the rebound.

CHAPTER 16

"So, how are things going with your father's estate?" Reid asked her. The evening breeze was cooler here on the beach, and the last orange-red rays of the sun were just disappearing over the horizon. Gentle waves rolled onto shore. He wasn't sure things could get more perfect than they were right now. Okay. Well, maybe one way they could get better: if Stacy agreed to stay in Boulder Point.

He'd packed them a gourmet picnic dinner with goodies from The Tuckaway and brought her back to their favorite spot on the rocks. His ever-awesome assistant, Bruce, had even managed to squeeze in a bottle of his best merlot and two glasses.

Stacy finished chewing a large bite of fresh lobster dipped in butter, swallowing before answering. "Good so far." She reached over and tapped her knuckles on the boulder beside her. "Knock on rock. All the major things have at least been started and the paperwork filled out. Now it's just a matter of waiting for everything to be processed."

"I'm glad." He sipped his wine and forked up some coleslaw. Homemade with Bruce's own tangy dressing. "What's your mom going to do now? Will she stay in the trailer or put it on the market?"

"Not sure yet. I'm guessing she'll stay, at least for a while. It's a good home, and she loves it, even if it is a bit big for just one person." She finished the last of her food then leaned back and sighed. "That was marvelous, as always. You are seriously a great chef."

"You say that like you're surprised." Reid gave her a side-glance and grinned. "I'm hurt. And you should be thanking Bruce, not me. He made all of this."

"Oh. Well, pass on my kudos to him," Stacy said, staring out over the ocean before them. "Remember the time in Home Ec when you tried to make stuffed flounder?"

He cringed. "I'm never going to live that down, am I?"

"Not in my lifetime," she teased. "Who knew fish could be so ... *flammable*?"

"Hey, I put it out before any damage was done."

Her serious expression dissolved into giggles.

"Thank goodness for the fire extinguisher."

"And the alarm. Don't forget that."

"How could I? Got us a whole afternoon off school." She shook her head, laughing. "The entire Boulder Point Fire Department showed up that day, I think."

"In my defense, things were slow around town," he said, shrugging.

This was nice. Sitting around, reminiscing about the past. He reached over and took Stacy's hand, lacing their fingers together before bringing them to his lips for a kiss. "And if I'm not mistaken, you were supposed to be watching the stove for me at that time anyway."

"Hey." She held up her free hand in mock surrender. "I never claimed to be an ace in the kitchen. And it didn't help that your friend Gabby was in the next kitchen over, making fun of me."

"True." He tugged her closer and wrapped his arm around her shoulders. The temperature had dropped a bit, and with the steady breeze, he didn't want her catching cold. Plus, it just felt so good to hold her and touch her. He couldn't get enough.

Part of him desperately wanted to just come right out and ask her to stay. After all, she could have a job lined up here with Ginny and the inn, and now with everything going on with her mother and family, Stacy had to at least have an inkling of how badly she was needed here at home.

The other part of him, though, was terrified he'd frighten her away once and for all. Even with so many things going for it, tiny Boulder Point was no match for the big city. And there was still the issue of Gabby. "Maybe you should try to talk to Gabby while you're here. She's changed a lot over the years, and now that she's married to Bruce, she's —"

Stacy gave a beleaguered sigh. "Seriously? Let's not ruin a beautiful night with thoughts of Gabby." She leaned back against him, her head resting comfortably against his chest as they watched the stars twinkle above. "I'm going to miss this when I leave."

His heart stumbled, and his breath hitched. Here was his opportunity to ask. Reid swallowed hard and forced the words past his constricted throat. "Do you think you could ever move back here?"

Stacy stilled, the only sounds around them the surf against the sand and the distant roar of traffic from the roadway above. She stayed silent so long that he wondered if she'd even heard him. He lived and died in that small eternity.

Then she took a deep breath and squeezed his hand. "For a long time after I left town, I thought I'd never return. After everything that happened between us and the way I was treated by some of the other kids after we moved to the trailer park, there was so much pain and resentment. Since I've been back, though, I've reconnected with my family ... and you. Honestly, I'm not sure what to do anymore. I've worked hard to build my career in Columbus. I'd be giving up a lot to move back to Boulder Point. I wish it was an easy decision, but it's not."

Hating the sorrow in her tone, Reid turned her to face him then tipped her chin up with his index finger. The hesitant look in her eyes matched the apprehension roiling inside him. She was afraid too.

He didn't want her to give up everything she'd gained for herself in Ohio, but he didn't want to lose her again. Perhaps it was time to take a chance, to put all his feelings on the table and tell her how he really felt. "Look, Sunshine. I —"

The buzzing of his phone interrupted his confession. Frowning, he pulled it from his pocket and squinted at the screen. His staff had strict instructions not to bother him tonight unless it was a true emergency, so whatever it was must be important. Gabby's name flashed on his caller ID. Even though he didn't want to let Stacy go, he had to take it.

"Who is it?" Stacy asked, leaning over to peer at his screen. "Nothing bad, I hope."

"It's the restaurant." He pushed to his feet and gave her an apologetic look. "Sorry, I need to take the call."

"Right. Sure." She nodded and looked out over the ocean. Reid's gut sank to his toes. He'd screwed up again, letting Gabby come between them. Stacy had seen his phone screen, he was sure. The phone buzzed for the third time, and he squeezed it tightly. A last glance at Stacy showed her resting her head atop her knees and staring out over the water, her expression pensive. Not good. Not good at all.

He walked several feet away and answered. "This better be life or death, Gabs."

"We've got a situation," Gabby said, aggravation prickling in her voice.

"What kind of situation?" Reid scowled. If this was another argument between her and Bruce, he'd seriously lose it. The most beautiful woman in the world was waiting for him on the rocks. He did not have time for Gabby's relationship woes. He'd given up so much already to keep her secrets safe; he wasn't sure how much more he could sacrifice.

"The dishwasher malfunctioned at the height of dinner service, and now we've got a sink-load of dirty plates and pans and about an inch of standing water on the floor."

Cursing, Reid ran a hand through his hair. "Okay. Here's what you need to do ..."

He rattled off a series of phone numbers for Gabby to call for help, then waited while she passed the phone to Bruce as she made the calls on another phone. Bruce relayed her progress, and in short order, they had a crew of human dishwashers on the way, the old appliance unplugged and waiting for the on-call plumber, and two sous chefs mopping the floor.

Impatient and on edge, Reid glanced back at Stacy and found her packing up their dinner, her frown darkening by the second. Damn, he shouldn't have taken the call! Couldn't Gabby have figured out how to handle that on her own without him bailing her out for once?

"I need to go," he said to Gabby after Bruce passed the phone back to her again. "You're going to have to handle things on your own from now on."

"Fine." Gabby snorted then stopped. "Are we talking about the restaurant or something more?"

"You know what I'm talking about, Gabs. It's time you started defending yourself. Stacy leaves Boulder Point in a few days."

"And?" Gabby said, her tone sharp.

"And I think you two have some business to settle. For my sake. You owe me, Gabs."

Her sigh echoed over the phone. "I'll think about it ..."

"Good," Reid said before ending the call. Once he got back to the rocks, however, Stacy had packed everything away and was waiting for him, looking disappointed.

"Sorry about that. Everything's under control again at the restaurant." He gestured toward the picnic basket. "We don't have to head back just yet, do we?"

"I'm tired," Stacy said, looking away. "I should get back to the inn."

She hopped down off the rocks, ignoring his offered hand. Reid caught her arm and turned her to face him, kissing her before he could think better of it.

"We still need to talk about things, Sunshine," he said, slipping his arms around her waist. "Boulder Point has a lot to offer you. The beach, your family. Me."

STACY'S HEART thumped so hard against her chest she felt sure Reid could feel it. Was he saying what she thought he was saying? Did he still feel about her the way she felt about him?

Her old doubts kept her from believing him. He'd

been quick to hide his phone, but not before she'd seen the caller ID. Gabby. Again. All her old insecurities rushed to the surface. What if she did stay? Would Gabby keep coming between them? And just what was Gabby's hold on him? She was married, for crying out loud, so why did Reid still jump when she called?

Stacy looked out at the ocean. Glimmers of light from the full moon just above the horizon danced on the waves. The sound of the surf was soothing. Her tension eased. That was the magic of the ocean that she had forgotten after all those years in Ohio.

Oddly enough, considering the sad circumstances over the last week, she'd been as happy and content as she'd ever been. Reconnecting with family and feeling as if she belonged. Funny, because when she first arrived in town, she couldn't wait to get back to Ohio. Now she didn't really want to leave.

"Look, I'm sorry about Gabby's call. It's not what you think," Reid said. "That was business."

The mention of Gabby's name brought a stab of hurt, but Stacy pushed it away. This was ridiculous. Whatever Reid had with Gabby must be over now. Otherwise, why would he be asking her to stay?

They started through the sand toward the stairs leading up to his truck.

"Stacy, please," Reid said, taking her hand again

and tugging her toward him. "I meant what I said. I'd love it if you moved back here and we could start over again fresh. From what you said earlier, I think you might like that too."

"Maybe. I have a lot to think about," Stacy murmured.

"At least tell me we can continue this conversation tomorrow."

Her heart squeezed as she turned to see the hopeful look on his face. "I'm sorry, I'm busy tomorrow. Girl day with my mom and Brenda." Stacy looked at him out of the corner of her eye, her lips quirking in a smile. "But maybe tomorrow night? I don't leave until the day after."

Reid's face broke into that charming grin that made her heart flip. "Sunshine, you've got yourself a date."

She waited for him to unlock the vehicle then slid into the passenger seat. Reid made her feel dreamy and hopeful and yearning for the future, but it wasn't guaranteed. Nothing was guaranteed in this life. Her father had taught her that. And she wasn't sure another chance with Reid was worth risking her heart again with so many unanswered questions — and Gabby — looming between them.

CHAPTER 17

S tacy woke early the next morning, realizing how childishly she'd acted about Gabby the night before. There had been a problem at the restaurant — of course Reid had to take the call. Even if it *was* from Gabby. She was his assistant, so naturally she'd be the one to call.

As she stared up at the sun-dappled ceiling, Reid's words kept looping through her mind.

Maybe if you talk to her ...

The thought of talking to Gabby again made her stomach knot. She'd taunted and teased Stacy relentlessly during school, especially after her father had lost his job.

For a long time, her parents had told Stacy to just ignore it, to cut Gabby some slack, seeing as how she didn't have a mother of her own, how she'd been raised by a father who was either drunk or working most of the time. But a lot of people grew up in those situations, and they turned out to be kind, generous, and wonderful.

Just look at Reid.

The firefly ring lay heavy on her chest, reminding her of the ten years she'd lost with her father while she'd pursued her career in Columbus. If only she could have one day of that back, one day to sit with her father and hear his sage advice. But he was gone, and she was left with only memories of him now. The last thing she wanted to do was make the same mistake again with her mother and her sister ... or Reid.

At the same time, though, she was terrified to talk to Gabby. What if she gave up everything she'd worked so hard for in Ohio only to come back home and fail in front of that woman again?

Regardless of what Reid and Ginny had said, she'd be starting all over. She'd have to find a place to live, get settled in at her new job at the inn, maybe even find extra gigs to supplement the income she'd lose by leaving the event company in Columbus. And there was no guarantee she'd be successful. And what about her and Reid? Would their feelings withstand the day-in, day-out rigor of constant contact?

She sat up and stretched. Maybe the smart thing to

do would be to ask for an extension on her leave of absence to try things out. She could fly back to Ohio tonight, talk to her boss tomorrow, and take a few days to settle her affairs and sign the necessary paperwork. That way she wouldn't burn any bridges or appear unprofessional. And maybe Ginny would let her try out the job at the inn to make sure they were a good fit for each other.

Downstairs, Stacy found Ginny in the kitchen with Maisie. Bacon sizzled on the stove, and the smells of freshly baked bread and strawberries filled the kitchen. Her stomach growled loudly as she took a seat at the table.

It was a good thing Maisie was cooking a big breakfast today, because Stacy was starving. She'd only eaten a few bites of lobster last night before Reid's phone call from Gabby ended the evening. "Anything I can help with, ladies?"

"Nope," Ginny said, smiling. "This is almost ready. Why don't you go on into the dining room, and I'll be there soon."

"Okay." Stacy did as she was told, taking a seat at the table she'd come to think of as hers and Ginny's. This was good. They'd have a chance to talk about the job here at the inn while they ate. A few minutes later, Ginny came in with two heaping plates of food. She set one in front of Stacy then took the seat across from her. "Thanks. This looks wonderful."

"You're welcome." Ginny eyed the salt and pepper shakers on the table warily.

"Something wrong?" Stacy asked.

"Oh, no. Nothing, dear. It's just ..." Ginny frowned then waved her hand dismissively. "It's nothing. Really. Everything's fine. What do you have planned for today?"

"Well, I was hoping to talk to you about the job offer, if it's still available."

"Yes, it's still available!" Ginny smiled, her expression surprised. "Are you interested?"

Stacy shrugged. "I might be. I'm considering my options. I'd like to do a trial run, if that works for you."

"Wonderful! We can try things for say, a month? If you like it and want to make it permanent, then you can go full time. Will that work?" Ginny spread home-made strawberry jam on a slice of toast. "You can even stay here while you're in town, unless you already have another place to live."

"I hadn't actually gotten that far." She gave a hesitant chuckle, realizing how ridiculous she probably sounded. "I'm still trying to decide if moving back here permanently is a good idea for me. Not all of my memories of living here are pleasant, and I just don't want anyone to think my coming home is a sign of failure."

Ginny scoffed. "Nonsense. Coming home would be a triumph. Because this time you'd be doing it on your terms, right? Besides, making more of yourself isn't about money or living in a fancy city. It's about being a success on the inside, about how you treat people."

"True." They ate in silence for several minutes, and Stacy continued to catch Ginny glancing at the salt and pepper shakers as if she expected them to jump up and dance a jig.

She wanted to ask her about why she was acting so strangely, but didn't want to intrude. Wasn't as if she'd been exactly herself lately either. Perhaps the stress of running the inn alone was getting to Ginny. In that case, Stacy coming to work here — even temporarily — would be a godsend.

Ginny finished her food and pushed her plate away. "Besides, I'm guessing you don't have any men as nice as Reid Callahan back in Ohio."

Stacy halted mid-chew.

"Being married to the right person makes life worthwhile too, you know."

Her heart twisted at the sorrow on Ginny's face. She'd seen that same look in her mother's eyes at

Dad's funeral. Honestly, Stacy had seen enough of that look to last her a lifetime. Still, doubts lingered about her and Reid. They'd gone on a couple of dates and kissed a few times. That was hardly serious enough to start thinking about marriage, right? She gave a nervous laugh and set her own empty plate aside. "I don't think Reid and I are anywhere near that stage yet."

"Hmm." Ginny sipped her coffee, watching Stacy over the rim of her cup. "Might be worth finding out, though, huh? And if it makes your decision any easier, I'll include the price of your room in your incentive package."

Stacy smiled. "That's very sweet of you. I booked a flight home tonight to see if I can work out the leave of absence with my boss, so I can't commit to anything until after I talk to him. The rental car company is picking up my vehicle this morning to fix the damage from my fender bender, but I'm spending the afternoon with my mom and sister at the salon. Is there a cab company or Uber in town I can contact to schedule a ride to the airport tonight?"

"I'm afraid Boulder Point isn't quite that hip yet," Ginny said, chuckling. "But I'll give Charlie Hanson a call. He runs the limo service here and can give you a ride. Maybe when you return from Ohio, the rental company will have the car back in shape and ready for you to drive again."

"Maybe." Seemed all the solutions to her problems were falling into place this morning. If only everything else in her life could be solved so easily. "I'll check in for my flight tonight and get my boarding passes before my sister picks me up this morning. Thanks again for your help."

"No problem," Ginny said, standing to collect their plates. "Glad to help."

INSIDE THE TUCKAWAY GRILL, Reid set up for lunch service alone. The restaurant didn't open for a few more hours, but he had two new catering clients coming in and wanted to have everything ready before they arrived. Both clients needed the same time slot today, so he'd booked one with Gabby and one with himself.

He was glad she seemed more settled now that things were okay again between her and Bruce. He needed a solid assistant in the business, and Gabby's drinking binges left him decidedly shaken. Things were back on solid ground again all the way around, and that was where he intended to keep them.

Now if he could just convince Gabby and Stacy to have their long-overdue talk, he'd be all set. It would make things so much easier and clear the path for him to convince Stacy that staying here with him in Boulder Point was right for her.

Last night, he'd been so close to swaying her; he could feel it. Then Gabby's call had ruined things, and Stacy had seemed even more distant when he'd dropped her off. Seemed he was back to square one again, all because of Gabs. He knew it wasn't her fault. She had no control over the actions of her parents any more than he did. They'd both just been kids when everything had gone down, but still.

It was time for Gabby to stand on her own two feet and accept and honor her past so they could all move forward together. He'd stand by her side, as he'd always done, because family came first — even the kind you didn't choose.

That knot of tension in his gut, the one that tightened ever so slightly each time he thought about Stacy leaving him again, squeezed harder. Ten years ago, he never would've considered leaving town to go after the woman he loved. Now he just might, if it meant having another chance with Stacy.

After all, he was older now. His priorities had

changed. He'd built the business he'd always wanted, but without love in his life, what was the point? He wanted a home, a family, a wife and a lover. He wanted more than just accolades for his food and balance sheets in the black. He wanted Stacy Brighton.

The front door opened, and Gabby walked in, smiling at him as she passed, talking on her cell phone. He watched her walk into her office before continuing to set up the other tables in the dining room. Once he was done, he grabbed silverware and centerpieces for the tables.

Gabby met him in the hallway. "Hey, I've been thinking about what you said last night."

"Yeah?" He filled a tray with knives, forks, and spoons, his pulse kicking a notch higher.

"Yeah. I think you're right. I should talk to Stacy. I owe her an apology after the way I treated her back in school."

He glanced over at Gabby and frowned. "Wow. That's a pretty big step for you, Gabs."

She shrugged. "I'm tired of holding all this inside me. And you're right. Times are different now. People change. Things don't carry the same stigma they used to. I'm a grown woman now, and it's time to put my big-girl panties on." She leaned in and kissed him on the cheek. "Thanks for being such a great protector all these years. I do owe you."

Reid gave her a self-deprecating grin. "Damn straight you do, Gabs."

"And I'm sorry about interrupting your date last night."

"Don't worry about it. It's fine."

"So, it was a date then, huh?" Gabby asked, an eyebrow raised.

"Maybe. I don't know." Reid picked up his now-empty tray and headed back to the storage room. Talking about his personal life wasn't something he usually felt comfortable with, especially when it came to Stacy. "You know things between us are complicated."

"Because of me." It wasn't a question. Gabby grabbed napkins and water glasses and began setting them out. "It's okay. And I'm sorry about that too. I never meant to cause you any more problems than I already have. Guess I need to talk to Stacy about that."

"No. I mean, yes, we do need to talk about that with her. But it's more than that now. She has a successful career in Columbus. I doubt she'd want to leave that to come here again, no matter what her feelings are toward me."

"And you have the restaurant."

"Yeah, for now."

"What does that mean?" Gabby asked, straightening. "Are you thinking about selling?"

"I don't know. I'm just trying to think through all my options." He finished putting out the silverware. "How would you feel about taking over managing this place if I decide to move to Ohio to be with Stacy?"

"Well, I'd certainly love to try, but isn't this a bit sudden?" Gabby crossed her arms and frowned. "Stacy's been back in town only a few days, and you guys are just getting to know each other again. Besides, I was going to ask for a week off to go on vacation with Bruce. We could really use the time away from everything to concentrate on the two of us and our relationship."

"Like I said, I want to cover all my bases just in case. And yes, to the week off. You and Bruce both deserve it."

"Great. Thanks." She checked her watch. "I hope our appointments show up on time. I've got a hair appointment at that new salon right after my meeting."

The sound of a car door slamming sounded outside, and Reid smiled as he shut off his cell phone. "Bet that's them now."

CHAPTER 18

The Tip Top Spa and Salon bustled with activity by the time Stacy, Brenda, and their mother arrived. Stacy joined them near the selection of polishes to select her color. "Hey, ladies. I know Mom's got her color already, but what are you getting, Bren?"

"Not sure," Brenda said, selecting a hot-pink color for her toes. "How about this one?"

"Oh, I like it!" She smiled and grabbed a bottle of sparkly red. The hue seemed appropriate given the changes she was about to make in her life — bold, daring. "I'm going with this one."

"How was your dinner last night with Reid?" her mother asked.

"Fine." She shook her head and took a seat in a nearby chair. "I've been making plans."

"With Reid?" Brenda asked, looking hopeful as she

plopped down in the seat beside her and shut off her phone.

"No. Oh, shoot! Hang on." That reminded Stacy she'd forgotten to check for Reid's answer to her earlier text. He'd sent a quick note saying he was thinking of her, and she'd replied by letting him know her plans had changed and she wouldn't be able to see him tonight after all, and then asked if she could make it up to him later.

She hadn't elaborated as to why. She still didn't know how her boss would react and didn't want to jinx the whole idea. And anyway, she wasn't sure she wanted Reid to think she was uprooting her life for him.

After all, she still wasn't sure where she stood with him, relationship-wise. Better to be safe than sorry this go-around. Besides, she'd rather tell him face-to-face and let it be a surprise, hopefully a pleasant one for him.

He usually responded quickly, so she kept her phone in her hand. Stacy sighed and turned to her sister again. "Please don't get too excited or read too much into this yet, but I've decided to ask for a longer leave of absence and give things here in Boulder Point a try. To see if I'd like to move back permanently."

"Oh, honey!" her mother gushed, taking the other

seat beside her and squeezing her hand. "That's wonderful! Is this because of Reid?"

"No, no. I told you, this is my decision. He doesn't factor into this at all."

She didn't miss the look her mother and Brenda exchanged over her lie.

Truth was, Reid did factor into this. How could he not, with their past and the potential future they might share? But he wasn't the entire reason. She hadn't realized until this week how much family meant. The thought of leaving them now tore her heart out.

And the town was quaint, peaceful. She'd missed that and the beach. She was tired of the hectic city life. Been there, done that. She'd proved she was a success. Now it was time to slow down. She was coming back for herself first. Reid was a very appealing added bonus. But it wasn't a decision to be made lightly, because if things didn't work out between them, she'd have to learn to get over it and move on.

"Well, I think it's great, sis. You'll be closer to your family. And this is a perfect place for a fresh start. Maybe moving back to Boulder Point could be another chance for you in a lot of ways."

"Let's hope so." She gave them both a tentative smile. "I'll be doing a trial run as the event planner at the Firefly Inn while I'm here. If things work out, I can work there full time."

"Wonderful." Her mother grinned. "I've got friends in the surrounding towns. They have daughters and granddaughters who'll need your expertise. I don't think you'll have any problems finding clients." She pulled out her phone and took a selfie of all three of them then posted it to her social media page with the caption "Goodbye, past. Hello, future!"

Stacy checked her cell again. Still no response from Reid.

She tried to not let it bother her. He was working today. Maybe he was busy. Maybe he was out of service range. *Or maybe he's with Gabby and is otherwise occupied.*

The niggle of doubt taking root in her stomach blossomed into full-blown anxiety. This was ridiculous. She was an adult, for crying out loud. She needed to talk to Gabby and clear the air.

The longer she put off talking to Gabby, the worse things would be, but she just couldn't bring herself to do it yet. All she wanted today was a few relaxing hours with her family before her flight home. There'd be plenty of time to have her conversation with Gabby when she returned, right?

"Three for pedicures?" a petite woman asked.

"Yes." They filed to the rear of the salon and took their places in the cushy recliners. Warm jasmine-scented water filled the sink below her, and jets of water massaged Stacy's feet as she enjoyed a back and neck massage courtesy of her chair.

The gentle technician and the experience helped ease some of her tension. Perhaps Reid was right. A decade had passed. They'd all matured. Maybe Gabby wasn't the same spiteful shrew she'd been in school.

Maybe she and Stacy could even become friends at some point. It would be nice to have another gal her own age to hang out with in town. The low volume of the television across from them, along with the occasional murmur of conversation from the attached hair salon next door, filled the silence.

Stacy leaned back and closed her eyes, enjoying the peace — until a familiar voice drifted through the doorway beside her. A decidedly female voice from her past that was etched in her brain forever.

"Reid wants to give me more — " Gabby said.

"What kind of pedicure would you like?" the technician asked, handing Stacy a menu and interrupting her eavesdropping. By the time she'd answered the tech's questions and given her back the menu, she'd missed a large portion of what Gabby had said to her stylist. Reid wanted to give her more what? Clients? Attention? Love?

"He said he wants to take things to a whole new level ..." Gabby continued.

Stacy's pounding heart now made it difficult to hear without leaning around the corner and being too obvious. She took a deep breath and closed her eyes, hoping to block out the rest of whatever Gabby was saying.

"... romantic vacation ..."

Ugh. Her pulse hitched, and her chest squeezed painfully. Reid wanted to take Gabby on a romantic vacation? Stacy opened her eyes and checked her phone screen again. Still no response.

Suddenly everything was different. Her plans to take a leave from her job and try Boulder Point weren't as appealing as they'd been a few hours ago. Stacy watched the technician with unseeing eyes, her mind whirling.

Was it really happening again? Reid choosing Gabby instead of her? Now she was unsure of her plans. Unsure of taking the job at the inn. Unsure of moving back to Boulder Point. The only thing she was sure of was that Reid Callahan had ignored her text, and she was leaving on the next plane back for Columbus.

"THANK you for choosing Callahan Catering. We'll talk again next week." Reid waved as his final set of clients pulled out of the lot. Gabby had finished long before he did and had gone on to her hair appointment.

There was still an hour before the lunch rush, though the bar, already open, was filled with regulars. He took a seat on an empty stool beside Charlie Hanson. He'd known old Charlie for years. In fact, they'd worked on several lobster boats together in the cove.

"Hiya, Reid," Charlie said, elbowing him in the arm. "I was just telling the guys here Dick Perkins caught a giant tuna today. Got it hanging down in the bait wharf right now."

"Wow! That's impressive this early in the season." Reid signaled his bartender for a glass of water. "And in Boulder Point!"

"Got that right." Charlie took a swig of his beer. "Used to see 'em all the time around these parts, but not so much anymore."

"Maybe I'll walk down there later and check it out." Reid smiled and pulled out his phone to switch it back on. A text from Stacy popped on his screen, saying her plans had changed and she probably wouldn't see him tonight, and asking if she could make it up to him later.

What the heck did that mean? Did it have something to do with Gabby's call interrupting their date? Was Stacy having second thoughts?

He frowned. Funny, except for the part about making it up to him, those were pretty much the last words she'd said to him before she'd left town ten years ago. Yelled them, actually. Right after he'd told her he couldn't leave and go with her to Ohio.

Boulder Point was home to everything he knew and loved — his father and brother, his life, his home. He didn't *want* to leave. Stacy hadn't understood that, hadn't trusted him enough to take his word.

Still, even with his heart broken and his future gone, Reid hadn't shared Gabby's secret. It wasn't his secret to tell.

This time, he prayed they'd both grown enough for her to believe in him now, at least until she and Gabby hashed things out. If not, there was no point in continuing things between them. He'd seen what a lack of trust had done to his parents. No way would he live the rest of his life like that, no matter how deep his feelings for Stacy.

He glanced at the phone again, a sinking sensation

in his chest. Was it happening all over again? Stacy slipping away as she did before? He should reply to her —

"Looks like old Dooley struck again," Charlie said, jarring Reid back to the present.

"Huh?" He looked away from his phone and frowned at the older man. "What's that?"

"Dooley. The ghost at the Firefly Inn. Looks like he sacred off the only guest." Charlie shook his head. "Feel bad for Ginny. She's real nice, but it's gonna be hard for her with a ghost rambling around."

Reid's frown deepened into a scowl. He really needed to see Stacy before she left, even if only to say goodbye.

"Ginny called me to schedule a limo pickup tonight for that young Brighton girl staying there. You probably remember her, Reid. In fact, I think you two went to school together. Stacy's her name. Pretty thing. Too bad about her dad. She's got an early flight back to Ohio, and my guess is she's not coming back this time." Charlie finished his beer and slid to his feet. "I need to get back to my boat if I'm going to get everything squared away before I need to pick her up. See ya later, Reid."

Stunned, Reid watched as the older man walked out of the bar before pulling out his phone once more.

He reread Stacy's message three times. *Plans have changed. Need to cancel tonight.* She'd agreed to go out with him tonight, but instead she was flying to Ohio. She was leaving him almost exactly as she had ten years ago.

CHAPTER 19

At four thirty that afternoon, Stacy was back in her room at the Firefly, shoving clothes into her suitcase without really paying attention to folding. Her concentration remained focused on the conversation she'd overheard at the salon. She'd originally planned to only go back for a day or so to talk to her boss, but now, after what Gabby had said, it looked as if she might as well return to Ohio for good.

She opened one of the dresser drawers and grabbed a handful of socks and underwear, cramming them in her bag before returning for another bunch.

How could she have been so stupid? She'd known from day one that Reid had a special attachment to Gabby, one she'd never been privy to. Why Stacy expected anything to be different now, she wasn't sure.

After all, she'd been gone ten years. Ten years in

which Reid and Gabby had had ample time to grow closer, to fall in love. Even if Gabby was married to his assistant. Tears stung her eyes, but she blinked them away hard.

Nope. She would not cry over this. She wouldn't.

Except she'd shared everything with Reid. He knew all about her family, her father's unemployment, everything. And still he'd not shared everything about his past with her.

She knew about his parents splitting up, of course, knew about his struggles growing up without a mother. But not once, not ever — even when they'd been as close as they'd ever been — had he told her what the deal was with Gabby. Seemed it was okay for Stacy to share her soul with *him*, but not the other way around.

It hurt. Worse than losing her father. Worse than losing their house when she'd been a child. Worse than anything, because she'd trusted Reid. Completely. Until now.

And now, the whole time he'd been romancing her, he'd been planning with Gabby.

She'd have to make up some excuse for her mom and sister as to why she'd changed her mind and wouldn't be temporarily moving back to Boulder Point, but that was a small price to pay to keep her sanity and her heart intact.

Maybe she'd tell them her boss begged her to stay. Maybe in a couple of months, after Reid and Gabby had returned from their fabulous romantic vacation and she was well and truly over him, she'd move back here and take the job Ginny had offered, just to spite him. Heck, maybe she'd even start her own event-and-catering company to give him a run for his money.

And Ginny, well, she'd just tell her the truth. That after careful consideration, she'd changed her mind, that the money and career potential in Ohio were just too enticing. That Boulder Point held too many memories and too much pain for Stacy to live here now.

A breeze ruffled the draft of the temporary resignation she'd printed on the desk under the window. Won't need that anymore.

She grabbed it in both hands, intending to rip it in half, but before she could make more than the tiniest tear, something jerked the paper from her hands. A shiver ran up her spine. That did not feel like a gust of wind. It was almost as if an unseen hand had grabbed the paper. Stacy watched as it hovered in front of her before it sailed out the window.

No!

She lunged for it, but it was already riding an air current away from the window. Shoot! She didn't want anyone to see what she'd written, and now it was drifting away. She leaned out the window, watching as it drifted over the cliff toward the private beach. Hopefully it would sink to the bottom of the ocean.

As she ducked back into the room, her neck chain caught on the window latch. The chain broke, her firefly ring slipping off and disappearing into the bushes below. Dang! Could this day get any worse?

This was a sign. A sign she was doing the right thing by leaving. She leaned farther out. Should she go down and try to find the ring? No. Her mother had given it to her in the hopes she'd have a happy, love-filled life like that of her parents. Fat chance of that happening now. Even though it had been her mother's ring, the fireflies reminded her of Reid. And she sure as hell didn't want to carry *that* reminder around the rest of her life.

She grabbed her bag and headed down to say goodbye to Ginny.

Her limo was due any minute, and she couldn't wait to get out of Boulder Point, once and for all.

REID WALKED DOWN THE BEACH, staring out at the ocean without really seeing it. This was the place he always came when he felt anxious or depressed.

Except tonight it was worse because all he could see now was Stacy. He climbed up onto the rocks where they'd first really connected after her return to Boulder Point and then later where they'd shared their first kiss and their picnic.

A large wave crashed against the rocks below, spraying him with water, and he jumped down onto the other side of the beach and continued onward. So many memories here, good and bad.

His mother used to bring him here as a kid, back before things got bad and she'd skipped town. They'd spend hours searching for starfish or tiny hermit crabs. Later, he'd come here after school with Stacy, looking for sand dollars and just talking about life.

Then there'd been the time he'd found Gabby here after her father had told her the truth about who her mother really was, that Reid was her half brother.

From that moment, things as they both knew them were never the same.

He'd wanted to tell Stacy about Gabby so many times, but obligation held him back. It wasn't his business to tell, and until his sister gave him permission, he felt bound to keep her trust. He only wished keeping her secret didn't cost him so much.

Reid nudged a piece of driftwood out of the way with his toe and sighed. He'd really thought this time, he and Stacy had a shot at forever. Yes, she'd been back only a short time, but they'd both grown so much, and he'd thought they were finally on the same wavelength. There was no denying the old feelings were still there. At least on his part.

Her change-in-plans text had rattled him. Had he moved too fast? Scared her off? Or had he only been a temporary distraction for her while she was in town? Maybe she had a boyfriend in Columbus and never intended to take things any further with Reid.

He stopped and stared up the side of the cliff, realizing how far he'd walked. That was the Firefly Inn up there. Was that a piece of paper floating on a wind current? Weird he'd never seen that before, and even weirder, it was heading straight toward him.

The paper whooshed by, and he reached out and snatched it out of the air. A wave crashed on the rocks, the sound mimicking the deep timbre of laughter. Reid whirled around, but no one was there. Just a trick of the rocks and waves.

He looked at the paper in his hand, his heart jerking when he read the words. It was Stacy's letter of resignation, asking her boss for three months off. The letter said she'd be there tonight to see her boss in person and tie up her projects.

She wasn't leaving town. She was staying! And

he'd ignored her text. What an idiot! He tugged his phone from his pocket and typed a reply. She could make it up to him any way she wanted.

He waited.

No answer.

Shoot!

He glanced up at the inn. If he hurried, he might be able to catch her before she left for the airport. Sprinting to the top of the rocks, he raced toward the stairs that led up the cliff to the inn.

Reid was out of breath by the time he got to the top. He stopped and rested for a minute with his hands on his knees, taking deep breaths to calm his racing pulse. If Stacy was still inside, he wanted to come across as calm and collected, not some wheezing buffoon.

After a few moments, he straightened and hurried up the path to the gardens behind the inn, his steps measured but his heart still racing.

Maybe he was wasting time. Maybe he should head straight to the airport. He didn't want to miss her, couldn't risk not telling her all the things he should have told her ten years ago.

He turned back toward the path down to the cliff-side and caught sight of something sparkling on the ground. Frowning, he walked over and bent down. It was a silver chain with a ring attached. His heartbeat stumbled like a drunken sailor. Stacy's chain. Stacy's firefly ring.

But why was it out here?

Straightening, Reid looked up at the second-floor windows. Could she have dropped it accidentally? He knew how much that ring meant to her. No way she'd leave it behind on purpose. She must still be here. He rushed to the front of the inn and knocked, the ring clutched tight in his hand.

Ginny answered on his third knock. "Reid Callahan? What are you doing here? Is something wrong?"

"I need to see Stacy," he said, out of breath again but for entirely different reasons this time. His pulse beat loudly in his ears, and he felt as if he didn't see Stacy, talk to her, tell her how he really felt right now, he'd never get another chance. "Please. Is she here?"

"Oh dear. I'm so sorry." Ginny's expression turned sad. "She left for the airport a few minutes ago. I'm afraid she's probably on her way back to Ohio by now. For good."

Time seemed to slow as the words sucker punched him in the gut. For good? The paper trembled in Reid's hand. "She's coming back, though, right?"

Ginny shook her head, a sad look on her face. "Sorry. She was but then changed her mind. Stacy really cares for you. That's probably part of the reason she's been so torn over making the decision about moving back here. She'd been all set until she got back from pedicures with her mother and sister, then she made an about-face. Said she overheard something at the salon that made her rethink everything. I tried to tell her not to jump to conclusions, to give Boulder Point another chance, but she wouldn't listen."

Reid cursed and ran a hand through his hair. Gabby had been at the salon earlier too. Had Gabby said something? If Stacy had overheard her talking and misconstrued something ... Panic overwhelmed him. "Right. I need to get to the airport."

"Yes, I think you do." Ginny shooed him away. "Go bring that girl home."

On the way to his truck, Reid pulled out his phone and sent a quick response to her earlier text, knowing it was too little, too late. But if she'd just see it, then maybe she'd have second thoughts about leaving.

Three little words.

Three little words that both terrified him and left him exhilarated.

Three little words that could change everything, if only she'd read them.

CHAPTER 20

Stacy sat at her gate at the airport, flipping through a copy of People she'd picked up in the gift shop, hoping it would keep her mind off of how hurt she'd been by what had happened with Reid.

She'd turned her phone off already, but because nothing she read in the magazine registered, maybe she should turn it back on and surf the web before she boarded?

Sighing, she tossed the magazine aside and closed her tired eyes. The week had passed in a blur. From day one, she'd been going, going, going. First the accident with Reid, then seeing her family again, then reconnecting with her hometown. The ache around her heart intensified, squeezing the air from her lungs.

Damn Reid and Gabby and their secrets.

She hadn't realized until this moment how much

she'd wanted to move back to Boulder Point and start a new life. Hadn't admitted to herself how badly she missed her mother and her sister and her nephew ... and Reid.

More tears stung her eyes, and she blinked them away hard, staring across the concourse at the endless sea of people hurrying to their destinations. A couple caught her eye in the gate across the aisle — they'd seemed so happy, laughing and talking and kissing. The woman looked up and caught Stacy's gaze, and her breath hitched.

Gabby. With a man who wasn't Reid. Must be hard juggling so many men at one time.

Was she having an affair already? Or was this the infamous husband Reid had mentioned? Was she going on a vacation with him too? A knot of doubt started to form in Stacy's chest. Something wasn't right.

She tried to look away fast, but it was too late. Gabby got up and walked to where Stacy sat, her smile tentative.

"Hello," she said, pointing to the empty chair beside Stacy. "Mind if I have a seat? I know I'm probably the last person on earth you want to see right now, but I think it's time we talked."

Stacy simply shrugged and looked away. There

was so much hurt between them, it would take a lot to heal the wounds. She doubted one talk would be enough.

"We haven't exactly been the best of friends ..." Gabby started.

Snorting, Stacy shook her head. "Got that right."

"Regardless, there are things about Reid and me that you should know." Gabby clasped her hands in her lap, her grip so tight her knuckles whitened. "I should've told you this a long time ago, knowing how close you and Reid were, but I was too ashamed. You're actually the first person I'm telling."

As you should be, Stacy thought. Cheating was an awful thing to do to someone, and who would be stupid enough to cheat on their husband with a guy they both worked with?

"After my mom died when I was ten, my dad was distraught. He loved her more than he loved life itself, and he couldn't cope once she was gone. He drank and spent most nights away from home. My mother was the best woman I've ever met — unselfish, kind, generous to a fault. As I've gotten older, I've done my best to be more like her. Putting other people's needs before my own."

That was it. Stacy couldn't hear any more. If Gabby was going to claim that she'd stolen Reid in high school as some sort of therapy or to help her heal and now they'd realized they still had feelings, she'd lose it. She gave Gabby a side glare. "This is very touching. I'm sorry for your loss, but does your story have a point?"

Gabby winced, and Stacy felt a sting of remorse before she shoved it aside. This woman had made her childhood a living hell, had bullied her and stolen the man she'd loved, not once but twice. The last thing she wanted to feel for Gabby Nelson was sorry.

"I deserved that," Gabby said finally, staring down at her toes. "Deserve more, I'm sure. I never got a chance to tell you, Stacy, but I'm so sorry for the way I treated you when we were kids. It's just that I was so jealous of you I could barely see straight. You were everything I wasn't — sweet, funny — everyone loved you, even Reid."

"I lived in the trailer park," Stacy said, the words harsher than she'd intended. Louder, too, if the stares they were getting from surrounding passengers were any indication. She lowered her voice and continued. "You had a fancy house in the best neighborhood. You were the most popular girl in school. Why in the world would you be jealous of me?"

"Because you were the one thing I could never be: authentic. You lived your truth every day. Me? I've been keeping secrets for so long now they're eating me up inside."

Bile rose in Stacy's throat, and she swallowed hard to keep it down as she forced words past her constricted vocal cords. "I don't really care if you're sleeping with Reid. Not this time, anyway."

This time it was Gabby's turn to snort, not in derision but in disbelief. "What?"

"You heard me. Don't act coy. You broke us up in high school. Congratulations. You did it again now. I don't know what this thing is between the two of you, but it's obviously stronger than whatever he feels for me. I can't compete." She cocked her head toward the man across the aisle who waited anxiously for Gabby's return. "Does he know you're seeing another man?"

"Stacy, I'm not sleeping with Reid."

"C'mon. I heard you at the salon earlier today. Taking about the romantic vacation he's taking you on and how you're reconciling."

Gabby laughed, the sound sad and mirthless. "I was talking about my husband, Bruce. Not Reid. The thought of sleeping with Reid is gross."

Defensiveness for Reid surged through Stacy's bloodstream, heating her cheeks and overriding her common sense. She swiveled in her seat to face Gabby head-on. "How dare you! Reid is the most decent, gorgeous, wonderful man I've ever known. You should feel honored to —"

"He's my half brother, Stacy."

It took a moment for Gabby's words to penetrate the red haze of Stacy's anger. When they did, the fire in her veins turned to ice, leaving her speechless. Then her words rushed out in a torrent. "Wait. You're telling me your dad slept with Reid's mom? Is that why she left town? Because she was in love with your father?"

"I honestly don't know," Gabby said, shaking her head. "All I do know is that it happened a long time ago and that my dad was ashamed of what happened. She was separated from Reid's dad. They'd been fighting a lot, and she was looking for comfort. She had me during the year they were separated and gave me to my dad right after I was born. My father told me that my mom couldn't have children and I was a gift. She set aside the fact he'd had an affair, and even though Reid's mom came back to his dad for a while, my parents avoided them. Of course, that didn't last long either. She eventually left Reid and his dad again, as you know."

Sorrow filled Stacy's heart. For all that had been lost. For everything they'd all been through because of that one night. One night had changed so many lives.

One night had taken away one person's options while giving so many others another chance.

"I asked Reid not to say anything after my father told me. And you know Reid. He's loyal to a fault. He kept his promise all these years. But I want to be more like my real mother now — the woman who raised me and cared for me, not my birth mother. Reid's mom never wanted me. She's never once even tried to contact me or them." Gabby sniffled. "Do you have any idea how worthless that made me feel? My own birth mother didn't want me. It's no excuse for how I acted toward you, but I was lashing out in the only way I knew how. I'm sorry you took the brunt of it."

Stacy slumped back in her seat, stunned. When she looked back now, so many things made sense. The way Reid had closed up whenever Stacy asked him about Gabby. The way Gabby always seemed to know just which buttons to push with Reid to get him to do what she wanted. The way Reid's family had always seemed cautious around Gabby and her father. No wonder Reid and Gabby had bonded; they shared the pain of a mother who abandoned them.

"I don't know what to say," Stacy said at last, her voice quiet.

"You don't have to say anything. I should've told you a long time ago. I'm truly sorry I didn't. I'm also sorry I let you live all these years believing I hated you and that Reid and I were a couple. It was so wrong, and I'm so, so sorry."

Stacy nodded, the weight of her resentment toward Gabby finally lifting, leaving her feeling freer and lighter but also untethered. If Reid wasn't sleeping with Gabby, that meant she *could* move back to Boulder Point, they could possibly have a life and a future together. If he still wanted her, if he still ...

"Flight 4206 to Columbus, Ohio, now boarding at Gate Six. Please have your boarding passes ready for the attendant," the announcer said over the public address system. Stacy gripped the paper in her hand tight, crinkling it.

Gabby reached over and took Stacy's hand, squeezing it reassuringly. "I've messed up a lot of things in my life, Stacy. I don't want you and Reid to be one more. My brother loves you. I know he does. If you care for him, then tell him. You're right. He's the best guy, and he deserves every good thing. He deserves to be happy, and you make him so happy, Stacy."

"What about your romantic vacation?" Stacy asked, still trying to take it all in. "You said at the salon he wanted to give you more, that he wanted to take things to a whole new level."

"Hey, honey." The man from across the aisle came over, his hands full of luggage. "They're getting ready to board our flight. You about done here?"

"Yes." Gabby smiled and stood. "Bruce, this is Stacy Brighton. She and I went to high school together. Stacy, this is my husband, Bruce Weaver."

"Nice to meet you," Stacy said, shaking the man's hand, her own still numb from everything going on. "Aren't you Reid's assistant at The Tuckaway?"

"I am." Bruce grinned. "Reid's my best bud."

"Yeah. He's told me great things about you."

"He should." Bruce chuckled, slipping his arm around his wife's waist. "I've saved his butt more times than I can count."

"Where are you going?" Stacy asked, the clouds in her head dissipating, leaving her mind racing. She should head back to Columbus and ask her boss for the time off. She should rush back to the inn and tell Ginny she'd take the job. She should run out of the airport right now and find Reid and tell him she loved him.

"Saint Croix." Gabby kissed Bruce's cheek, taking the handle of her wheeled suitcase from him. "Time for some couples R and R. Oh, and about those things you heard? Reid was talking about you. He was thinking about having me take over as manager of The

Tuckaway so he could move to Columbus and be with you if you refused to move here. And the romantic vacation? That was for me and Bruce."

"It was nice to meet you, Stacy," Bruce said, waving as he led Gabby back across the concourse to their gate.

"Yeah, you too," she said absently. Reid was willing to give up his career, the life he'd built, and move across the country just to be with her. Maybe Ginny was right. Maybe this was another chance for them to be together. If she was brave enough to take it.

"Last call for Flight 4206 to Columbus, Ohio, at Gate Six," the announcer said.

Stacy's heart raced. Stay or go?

Run again or face the man she loved and fight for what she truly wanted?

In the end, there was no choice.

She grabbed her carry-on suitcase and raced for the exit.

REID RAN into the brightly lit atrium of the Portland International Jetport and scanned the crowds of people in the area. No sign of Stacy. His heart fell.

He'd hoped to catch her before she went through

the security checkpoint. He stared at the arrivals-and-departures screen in time to see the flight to Columbus tick from "boarding" to "departed." Through the floor-to-ceiling glass along one wall of the lobby, red lights flickered from the tail end of a jet as it soared into the sky. So much for his grand gesture.

He slumped back out to his truck and climbed behind the wheel. Normally, when things were crappy and he just wanted to get away for a while, he went to the beach. But now there were so many memories, too many memories, of Stacy there for him to feel anything but anxious among the rocks and waves.

Dinner service at The Tuckaway would be almost over by now. He decided to head back there instead and help the crew clean up. He'd left the fill-in sous chef in charge because Bruce was on vacation with Gabby. The kid was fresh out of culinary school and still learning when it came to hands-on business experience, but he was a capable enough manager. Bruce seemed to have taken a liking to him, acting as a sort of mentor.

His mind wandered to Stacy once more as he drove. He hoped she had a good flight back to Ohio, hoped she got things settled at work. But more than anything, he hoped she'd find it somewhere within her heart to forgive him. He smacked his hand hard against the steering wheel and cursed. He should've told her about Gabby being his sister. Would she ever forgive him for not telling her?

Sighing, he slowed for the red light and ran a hand over his face. Reid was done keeping secrets, done with holding things inside until they nearly ripped him apart. From now on, he'd tell the truth and let it run where it would.

The light turned green, and he turned down the road toward The Tuckaway. A light drizzle started, making the roads slick and fogging his windshield. He flipped on the wipers and squinted out the cleared space but still couldn't see well. Seemed one of the streetlights near the cemetery had burnt out. He'd have to say something to the mayor the next time she came in for dinner.

Distracted, he nearly didn't see the compact car stopped along the side of the road until it was too late. Reid slammed on his brakes and skidded to a halt behind the car, which was running with the lights on but appeared to be parked. A quick glance showed a rental sticker on the back bumper.

Great. More tourists causing mayhem on the roadways.

Scowling, he honked at the driver to move but got no response.

The rain pelted down harder, and he mumbled under his breath about idiot drivers and reckless behavior before turning on his truck's hazard lights and climbing out. Shoulders hunched and collar up on his jacket to keep dry as best he could, he headed for the driver's-side door. On the off chance that the driver was in trouble, his conscience required him to check.

Reid knocked on the window and waited as the tinted glass slowly lowered to reveal the last person he expected to see.

Stacy.

Stunned, he stepped back as she peered up at him, her eyes and nose red from crying.

She sniffled, her tears flowing harder now. "My dad's in there, Reid." She pointed to the cemetery with a shaking finger. "He's dead, and he never got to do all the things he wanted to, and I never got to say goodbye, and I'm sorry. I'm just so sorry ..."

Her words trailed off as her sobs grew stronger.

Finally, Reid snapped out of his fog and reached for the handle of her car door. "Get out."

"W-What?" she hiccupped between sobs.

"Get out of the car, Stacy." He kept his voice deliberately calm and gentle, despite the overwhelming urge to sweep her into his arms and never let her go again. "Please."

She grabbed a wad of tissues from her purse on the seat beside her then slowly undid her seat belt and exited the car. After wiping her eyes and nose, she leaned back against the wet vehicle and stared at her toes. "I saw Gabby, at the airport. She told me the truth, about your mom. So she's your sister, huh?"

Her statement lifted a weight from Reid's shoulders, and he took her hand, needing to touch her, needing that connection. "I wanted to tell you so many times, Stacy. I did. But it wasn't my secret to tell, and —"

"I know." She squeezed his fingers reassuringly. "I understand now. And I commend your loyalty to your family and those you love. It's one of the things I love most about you."

"I'm glad Gabby's decided to come out with it after all these years. I tried to tell her that —" Stacy's words penetrated the whirling thoughts in his head and stopped him short. "What did you say?"

Stacy looked up at him through her lashes. "I said I commend your loyalty to your family. Family is really important. I want to stay close to mine from now on."

"No." He moved closer to her warmth and tipped her chin up with his finger, loving the feel of her soft skin. "After that?"

The sparkle in her eyes deepened into something

warmer as they stood in the glow of his truck's head-lights, droplets of rain glimmering like diamonds around them in the summer night. "Oh. You mean the part about me loving you?"

"Yeah, that's the part I mean." Unable to resist any longer, he captured her lips with his in a sweet kiss. She tasted of coffee and cinnamon and home. When he finally pulled away, his arms were around her waist and her hands were around his neck. Reid rested his forehead against hers and smiled, so grateful he'd gotten another chance with the woman he loved. "I've got something for you."

"You do?" Stacy leaned back, her expression quizzical.

"Are you missing something?"

She frowned. "No. I don't think so." She patted herself all over, stopping over her chest. "Oh right. My necklace. The one with my mom's ring. It fell out the window. I thought I didn't want it, but ..."

Fresh tears welled in her eyes, and he couldn't bear it a second longer.

"Well, it just so happens that I found this earlier." He pulled the ring from his pocket and held it up between them. "Sorry to say your chain is broken." He took her hands and slid the ring onto her finger. "But I think it fits just fine here."

"Reid." Stacy gave him a watery smile. "Does this mean what I think it does?"

"That I love you more than I can ever say? Yes. It does. If you'd checked your texts, you'd have seen it." He gathered her close once more, kissing the top of her head. "Now, about you flying back to Columbus …"

CHAPTER 21

One week later...

Pinks and golds streaked the horizon above the ocean as the lazy summer sun sank behind Maine's pine forests. Ginny stood at the kitchen sink and watched Reid and Stacy holding hands on the deck. They seemed to be enjoying that new settee with the fancy canvas cushions she'd bought as they sipped their wine and took in the gorgeous sunset. In front of them, a few early fireflies began to blink, their glow not nearly as bright in the dim shades of dusk.

She smiled and turned her concentration back to the strawberries she was washing for Maisie to use the next day. Tomorrow's breakfast menu included scones and pancakes.

Things had worked out all right. Stacy had accepted the job as event planner at the Firefly Inn —

in no small part, Ginny was sure, due to Reid. The two of them had been inseparable since Stacy had returned to Boulder Point. Stacy had secured the okay from her boss in Columbus to take a six-month sabbatical from her job in Ohio and had packed a few more of her things to bring back to Maine.

Instead of moving back into her room at the inn, however, she'd decided to stay with her mother at the trailer park. Not that she'd be there long either, if the way Stacy and Reid clung to each other was any indication. That was good for Ginny too, because the Firefly Inn was booking rooms faster than she could clean them.

After placing the container of clean berries in the refrigerator, Ginny peered out the French doors at a still-full bowl of cat food. She'd not seen her nocturnal guest since that night with Stacy, but she had heard him meowing.

Experience with felines or not, she couldn't stand the thought of the poor thing starving. The cat still hadn't touched the food, but maybe that was a good thing. Maybe some other kind person had taken him in, and she wouldn't have to worry about him becoming dependent upon her.

The gardens looked better. Ginny had worked out there most of the morning, trying to get them in shape for the upcoming wedding party. She'd cleared most of the overgrowth and brush from between the beds but still needed to make a run to the garden center in Portland for fresh flowers and to fill in the sparse spots. Maybe she should consider hiring a gardener or at least someone part time to keep up with the work.

Ginny turned back to the sink to find the salt and pepper shakers sitting on the windowsill. Shaking her head, she grabbed them and walked to the table, ready to place them in the center once more until a booming male voice stopped her cold.

"Madam! If you don't stop moving those shakers, I will not help you with your endeavor."

Shaking, Ginny whirled around but found no one. She clutched the tiny porcelain shakers tightly and sank into one of the chairs at the table.

Maybe it had been a trick of the mind. She'd been working extra hard lately and was stressed about the big wedding coming up. Stacy should help with some of that anxiety, as should the lawn crew she had coming in to get the grounds into shape this weekend. But maybe it had all gotten to her more than she'd thought.

That had to be it.

The voice had been a figment of her imagination, perhaps a little too much sun earlier in the day.

Still, she put the shakers back on the windowsill, just in case.

****

GET emails for all of Annie Dobbs latest sweet romances:

http://anniedobbs.com/newsletter/

JOIN ANNIE/LEIGHANN'S private readers group on Facebook:

https://www.facebook.com/groups/ldobbsreaders/

WOULD you like a text whenever Annie releases a new romance? Text ROMANCE to 88202 (sorry, this only works for US cell phones!)

ALSO BY ANNIE DOBBS

Sweet Romance

Hometown Hearts Series

***

No Getting Over You (Book 1)

A Change of Heart (Book 2)

Magical Romance with a Touch of Mystery

***

Something Magical

Curiously Enchanted

****

Romance and Cozy Mystery - Written as Leighann Dobbs:

Romantic Comedy

***

Corporate Chaos Series

In Over Her Head (book 1)

Can't Stand the Heat (book 2)

Contemporary Romance

***

Reluctant Romance

Cozy Mysteries

Lexy Baker Cozy Mystery Series

* * *

Lexy Baker Cozy Mystery Series Boxed Set Vol 1 (Books 1-4)

Or buy the books separately:

Killer Cupcakes

Dying For Danish

Murder, Money and Marzipan

3 *Bodies and a Biscotti*

Brownies, Bodies & Bad Guys

Bake, Battle & Roll

Wedded Blintz

Scones, Skulls & Scams

Ice Cream Murder

Mummified Meringues

Brutal Brulee (Novella)

No Scone Unturned

Cream Puff Killer

Mooseamuck Island Cozy Mystery Series

* * *

A Zen For Murder

A Crabby Killer

A Treacherous Treasure

Mystic Notch

Cat Cozy Mystery Series

* * *

Ghostly Paws

A Spirited Tail

A Mew To A Kill

Paws and Effect

Probable Paws

Silver Hollow

Paranormal Cozy Mystery Series

***

A Spell of Trouble (Book 1)

Spell Disaster (Book 2)

Nothing to Croak About (Book 3)

Cry Wolf (Book 4)

Blackmoore Sisters

Cozy Mystery Series

* * *

Dead Wrong

Dead & Buried

Dead Tide

Buried Secrets

Deadly Intentions

A Grave Mistake

Spell Found

Fatal Fortune

Western Historical Romance

***

Goldwater Creek Mail Order Brides:

Faith

American Mail Order Brides Series:

Chevonne: Bride of Oklahoma

ABOUT THE AUTHOR

Annie Dobbs is the pen name of USA Today Best-selling author Leighann Dobbs. Leighann discovered her passion for writing after a twenty year career as a software engineer. She lives in New Hampshire with her husband Bruce, their trusty Chihuahua mix Mojo and beautiful rescue cat, Kitty. When she's not reading, gardening, making jewelry or selling antiques, she likes to write cozy mystery and historical romance books.

Her book "Dead Wrong" won the "Best Mystery Romance" award at the 2014 Indie Romance Convention.

Her book "Ghostly Paws" was the 2015 Chanticleer Mystery & Mayhem First Place category winner in the Animal Mystery category.

Get emails for all of Annie Dobbs latest sweet romances

http://anniedobbs.com/newsletter/

If you want to receive a text message alert on your cell phone for new releases, text ROMANCE to 88202 (sorry, this only works for US cell phones!)

Join Annie/Leighann's private readers group on Facebook:

https://www.facebook.com/groups/ldobbsreaders/

9 781946 944498